For Rasal

C000262072

About the author

R.F. Moore is a UK-based writer specialising in technical writing and editing. His other life is fiction writing, and this is the third of a series of novels featuring Inspector John Keane. He has also written the lyrics for a large number of songs with varying degrees of success, and has even won prizes for his poetry.

R.F. Moore

Also by R.F Moore

Journey to Nowhere

End of the Line

Something Special

Crimes from the Hidden City

www.rfmoore.com

For Rosalind...

R.F. Moore

R.F. Moore
The Closed Affair

"In a closed circle of friends, when envy and pride collide, there is bound to be a death sooner or later."

Raymond Chandler

Ahead Publishing

This edition, with revisions, published by *Ahead Publishing* in 2018
The right of R.F. Moore to be identified as the author of this work has been
asserted in accordance with the Copyright, Designs and Patents Act 1988.

Dedication

To Joni Mitchell, whose first album was dedicated to her Grade 7 English teacher,
Mr. Kratzmann, "... who taught me to love words."
She did the same for me.

Musical Acknowledgements

Lyric extracts in chapter headings are from the accompanying CD *'The Closed Affair'.*
The songs were inspired by the relevant chapter in the book - either directly or
indirectly – and are a commentary on the characters and events in the book.

Vocals: Tim Philips and R.F. Moore. Backing vocals: Keith Hughes.
Guitars: Gavin Redshaw. Saxophones and Flute: Tim New.
Programmed drums, bass, guitar and piano: John Bridges.

Special thanks to Keith Hughes for the collaborations that inspired
Respectable and *Our Little Girl.*

All lyrics and music on the CD © R.F Moore.

ISBN: 978-0-9566170-2-6

Design and typesetting by Graphicgene   www.graphicgene.co.uk.
Printed by Book Printing UK.

Characters

in order of appearance

Col Templemead-Newson	Retired Indian Army Officer
Mr & Mrs Ruane	Parents of Lizzie Steet
Detective Inspector John Keane	Police Officer
Jim Steet	Husband of Lizzie Steet (née Ruane)
Tristan Thorpe	Art Dealer
Matthew & Priscilla Parry	Eminent Surgeon and his wife
Ray & Jilly Raymond	TV Producer and TV presenter
Mr & Mrs Chadra	Diplomats stationed in the UK
Frances Hawkins	Novelist
Detective Sergeant Wilshire	Police Officer
Lizzie Steet (née Ruane)	Deceased

Tristan Thorpe

Mr & Mrs Ruane

LODGE ROAD

THE GRANGE

Matthew & Priscilla Parry

Colonel Templemead-Newson

Ray & Jilly Raymond

MANOR PARK DRIVE

Mr & Mrs Chadra

Frances Hawkins

PARK MANOR

GATES

HILLSIDE ROAD

Jim Steet

Inspector Keane Police Station

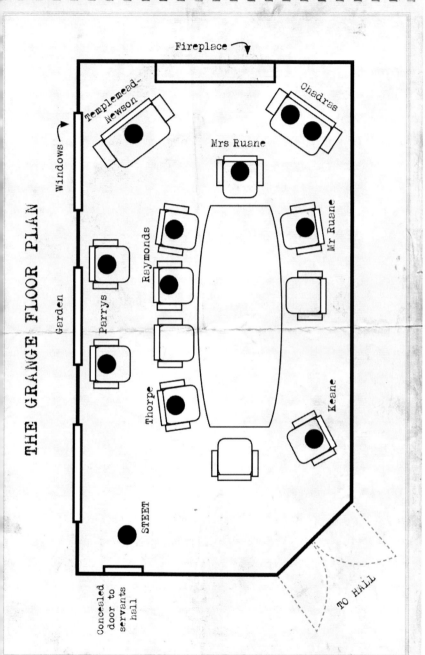

THE GRANGE FLOOR PLAN

Fireplace

Windows

Garden

Templemead-Newson

Chadras

Mrs Ruane

Mr Ruane

Parrys

Raymonds

Thorpe

Keane

STEET

Concealed door to servants hall

TO HALL

The Closed Affair

Late autumn 1969, and Inspector John Keane gets an invitation to a reunion with old colleagues. But when he reaches the house, his fellow guests are not the ones he expected. Then a man with a gun suddenly appears. Convicted of his wife's murder and sentenced to life, he has escaped and ensnared all of those involved. He will now find the real killer. Keane must act as investigator and judge, and when the verdict is announced, the gunman will be the executioner. Then the ghosts of the past will be laid to rest and the victim avenged.

CHAPTER 1
A face from the past

The beginning of the story

The judge and jury in their seats
The warders with a prisoner each
Who will sort the truth from lies
When truth is hiding from their eyes

"Damn'd funny dinner party, if you ask me," growled the Colonel. "No host here to greet us? Dashed bad manners, I call it."

He looked around at the other guests and scowled. Colonel Templemead-Newson's scowl was something that, in years past, had scared many an upstart young officer in his regiment. But this evening it was directed toward the other guests sitting in the dining room of The Grange.

Mrs Ruane looked equally discomforted. It was strange for her to go back into their old house after what had happened there. They had sold it after the death of their daughter. But previously it had been the Ruane's house - and before that her grandparents and then her parent's house - from the time it had been built in the 1850s.

"Well," growled the Colonel, "Let's not shilly-shally, I assume we all received the same invitation to come to dinner at The Grange tonight?"

They all nodded.

"So, where is our host? What's the fellow's name? Ah, yes, John Keane. Don't know him myself. Only came because this place is next door to me and I wanted to see what the new owners had done to the place. Never been in the place since they bought it. Never got an invite when they moved in. And never hear a peep from them or see anyone going in or out. Very mysterious, I call it."

He looked round. "Doesn't seem to have changed much. Still the same decor as when …"

"… When we lived here," interrupted Mrs Ruane hurriedly. The events of that terrible day were never discussed in her presence. But that did not put the Colonel off his stride.

"Damn shame what happened. Your daughter was a fine girl. Used to come and sit with me whenever I had a bad turn with the malaria. Never goes away, y'know, even though it's many years since my days out East. Yes, my time in India still comes back to haunt me."

He looked across the room to Mr Chadra, suddenly feeling embarrassed. "No offence meant, old chap. Dashed nice people … good soldiers too. Had some excellent enlisted men in my regiment in Ahmedabad. But the climate is not for us the likes of us. No ..."

He stopped abruptly as the door into the dining room opened and a newcomer came into the room.

There was an uncomfortable silence as the new guest limped slowly towards the large dining table in the centre of the room. He was leaning heavily on a walking stick. He looked around, clearly puzzled.

"Good Evening. I am John Keane. I was …"

"At last," interrupted Mrs Ruane. "Our mysterious host! But I don't believe we have ever met, Mr Keane?"

Keane looked at her and, suddenly, had an ominous feeling that this was not going to be the reunion with a few ex-colleagues that the invitation he'd received a few days ago had promised.

A wealth of memories came flooding back to him. Mrs Ruane was the mother of Elizabeth Ruane.

And Elizabeth Ruane had been murdered in this house – in fact in this room. He tried to remember the exact date … it must have been around five years ago.

He cleared his throat. "Oh, we have met, Mrs Ruane. I am Detective Inspector John Keane …"

A new, harsher voice interrupted him. "… Detective Chief Inspector John Keane. Let's get your title right now you've got your promotion. Surely you will remember him now, Mrs Ruane. Or is your memory even worse than it was at the trial?"

At the sound of his voice, everyone in the room looked up in surprise. They saw a man who had appeared in the far corner, seemingly from nowhere. In fact, he had made his dramatic entrance from a concealed door in the far wall used by the servants to bring in food for the grand dinners held in the days of Mrs Ruane's Victorian relatives.

The man was probably quite young, but he was prematurely aged with a lined face and hints of grey in his dark hair.

He stood quite still, an intense expression on his face. And in his hand was a lethal-looking automatic pistol.

He spoke in a calm, controlled voice. "I am glad you were all able to join me here – it would have been a shame to have left anyone out. A great shame. 'Cos I need you all here to finish what you all started. "

Keane looked at him more closely and realised he knew the man. It was Jim Steet, who had been convicted of the murder of his wife Elizabeth - the only daughter of the Ruanes - in a particularly unpleasant and notorious case. Steet was sentenced to be hanged at one of the last trials when capital punishment was still on the statute books.

His death sentence had eventually been commuted on the grounds of diminished responsibility by the Appeal Court. He'd had a climbing accident shortly before the murder, and his newly-appointed legal aid Counsel, backed by an eminent psychiatrist, successfully argued that the accident had upset his balance of mind at the time of the murder. So Jim Steet's sentence was commuted to life, with little hope of an early parole.

However, Mr and Mrs Ruane, had been vociferous in a campaign to have the reprieve overturned and Steet hanged. This was a legal impossibility anyway, and made more pointless by the fact that in the meantime hanging had been all-but-abolished. Though Keane remembered that it had, rather bizarrely, been retained for the crimes of mutiny by a member of the armed forces and few other obscure offences. But the Ruane's vindictive campaign helped to keep the wounds of her murder open even longer.

The Ruanes, along with their daughter, had lived in their large Victorian house on this exclusive private estate accessed along a gated road. It was a very closed and closeted community, with all the residents knowing each other and all their lives tightly intertwined.

Indeed, there was local gossip at the time that Elizabeth - or Lizzie as everyone but her parents called her - was having an affair with one of the neighbours in the street.

Mrs Ruane was the first to speak after Jim Steet's dramatic entrance. "But you are in prison. Serving life - and that is only because the misguided Appeal Court Judges commuted your death sentence. You shouldn't be here at all - you should have been hanged long ago." There was a trace of hysteria in her voice.

"Oh, yes. That was what you wanted. But you are right in one respect - the Appeal Judges did save me from the gallows once they saw how flimsy the evidence was." The gun was steady even if his voice was not.

"But I learned a lot of things in prison over the last few years and made a lot of friends. Even criminals don't like someone being framed. It hurts their professional pride. So two lifers planned an escape and took me with them. The other two are a fair way from here now, but I stayed around.

"And let me tell all you why I stayed."

He looked round the table at the frightened people tricked there by his invitation.

"I am going to conduct another trial – a proper one this time. And I will find out who really murdered Lizzie."

Jim Steet looked round the room at the assembled guests. "I think it is up to me as your host – a nicer word than captor, I think – to introduce you all. More for the Inspector's benefit than yours."

He laughed, "No, you do not need introducing to each other. Part of the problem was that you all knew each other too well … far too well, I suspect. But that is for the Inspector to find out.

"So, Inspector, I can see that you remember Mr and Mrs Ruane all too well. And I doubt if you could ever forget Colonel Templemead-Newson."

The Ruanes did not acknowledge the introduction, while the Colonel nodded at Keane as if he was meeting a brother officer from a Regiment newly arrived at the front.

"Do you remember any of the others, Inspector?"

Keane looked around the room. "Yes. If I am correct, over there are Ray and Jilly Raymond along with Matthew and Priscilla Parry, Tristan Thorpe, and … the lady from the far end of the street. Miss Hawkins, I believe."

She smiled. "A good memory for names, Inspector Keane. That must be a most useful attribute to have as a detective."

Keane smiled back at her – he remembered she had been helpful when he had been taking the first statements, before the Yard took over the investigation from him. A sharp eye and a sharp mind.

He did remember the final couple who were sitting rather aloof in the corner by the window, but despite Miss Hawkin's compliment, their names eluded him.

"Mr and Mrs Chadra, the Indian diplomat and his wife." Steet helped him out.

"They were not here for long, just passing through, so you can be forgiven that lapse."

Mr Chadra raised his hand slightly, while his wife looked at Keane in a near-hostile way for a reason he could not fathom.

Jim Steet continued his narrative. "I have a jury ready for the trial with all of you here, and I invited Inspector Keane to be the Judge. While I shall be the executioner of the guilty one." He looked down for a second at the pistol.

"You might think that you can escape or overpower me. And Inspector Keane would maybe have stood a chance if he had been fit.

"But he is not - look how he limped in here like an old woman. You see, the Inspector had a little unplanned swimming lesson from the Paterson gang and has not recovered yet."

Steet laughed and pointed at Keane's stick. "The police

chase car with the Inspector inside ended up in one of the lakes on the Heath when pursuing Jas Paterson's Cortina. Keane was lucky to get out alive, but Jas wasn't so lucky - they found the body a few days later - but haven't found the loot so far."

Keane looked down at his injured leg - it still was painful if he tried to walk too much. "You seem very well-informed Steet, especially for a man who has been in prison for most of the past few years."

Steet frowned at the memory. "Oh, I used my time in prison well, Inspector. Anyway, the prison bush telegraph is often better-informed than the newspapers or the radio and TV about criminal affairs. And as you might imagine, there is plenty of time on your hands to read and to learn useful things.

"I'll give you an example. In the prison library I learned about weapons – how to get hold of them and how to use them effectively."

He lifted the pistol a little and laughed. "You wouldn't think a prison library would be so foolish to have allowed such books. But I simply ordered my regulation two books a month from the prison librarian and no one checked to see what they were really about!

"And if any of you were thinking of excusing themselves from this re-trial, I should explain that when the Ruanes sold this house, as Keane knows, it was bought by the Government for various purposes.

"And it was discreetly but carefully made very secure so that no one can get in – or out – unless they are allowed to.

"I will not allow any of you to leave – or anyone outside to get in - until I have discovered the truth behind all the lies - and find out who really killed Lizzie.

"So you see, you have no choice other than to stay and

take part in my new trial - the one that will find the truth. You are going to be my jury and you will have to do better than the lot at the first trial. "

Keane looked around the room: "There are only eleven here. You need twelve for a jury."

"Well spotted, Inspector."

Jim Steet pulled a notebook from his pocket. "Here is our twelfth jury member. It is Lizzie's diary. It was hidden from me, but now I have it! As well as its sentimental value to me, it also contains a few revelations that some of you would prefer are kept under wraps."

He pushed it back in his pocket. "Yes, she is our final jury member. So we have a crime, we have a jury, we have a judge and …" he smiled, but it was a thin and cold smile as once again he raised the pistol slightly for emphasis.

"… and we have an executioner. Yes, I think we are ready to begin."

Keane realised then that Steet was going to make all eleven plead their case. Plead for their lives. For there was no doubt that he would kill the guilty one – and anyone who tried to escape.

When he received the invitation, Keane had been intrigued. Of course, he knew the house from his brief involvement in the investigation at the time. But although he had arrived on the scene as the CID local officer on the spot, he had rapidly been replaced by members of the Scotland Yard Murder Squad, as was the usual procedure.

The case – as he remembered it – had been fairly cut and dried. Posh local girl takes up with local lad from the other side of the tracks – in this case other side of the main road – and starts a liaison that is totally opposed by her parents. After a quick wedding, all goes wrong and the arguments start … ending in a final violent quarrel and the death of the girl.

The parents – Mr and Mrs Ruane – testified to increasingly violent arguments as their daughter started to realise her terrible error. They explained at the trial that Jim Steet had enrolled her as a model and used her substantial earnings to subsidise his own dissolute lifestyle. But by then it was too late for her to escape from him.

The case ended as expected with a straightforward trial, cast iron evidence, a quick three-hour guilty verdict from the jury and the black cap donned by the Judge – probably one of the last times he would do that.

Keane stood silent, looking round the room and remembering it as the place where the girl's body had been found. Nothing much had changed as far as he could remember.

It was a typical dining room for these turn-of the-century houses. Large with oak-panelled walls. High, wide windows and the obligatory neo-stately-home grand fireplace at the end of the room. The room was an important part of such Victorian homes where a large family with their dinner guests would sit round the table for a formal meal as servants brought a huge succession of courses.

The only off-key note was that the windows were securely boarded-up so that no one could possibly get in - or out for that matter.

The dining room still had the large table in the centre with a set of heavy leather chairs arranged round it. There were also two settees at the far side of the room with intricate flower-patterned covers. The large marble fireplace that had once been the centrepiece of the room now contained just a miserable electric fire with an artificial flame effect doing its best to give an impression of warmth.

It was all very old-fashioned and out of date, but

Keane assumed that the new owners had left the room unchanged as it suited them to have somewhere traditional where a large group could sit and dine together.

This was the setting for Jim Steet's re-trial, an appropriate one, Keane reflected, as the site of the murder. Looking round, he tried to think back and refresh his half-forgotten knowledge of those now trapped in the room, enticed by Jim Steet's invitations.

On his right, sitting on three of the leather-clad dining chairs, were Mr and Mrs Ruane and Tristan Thorpe, the art dealer from the house opposite. On the other side of the room on four more chairs were Matthew Parry, an eminent heart surgeon from the other house opposite, with his wife Priscilla. Next to them, Ray and Jilly Raymond, who both worked in television.

Sitting together on the small settee in the corner were Mr and Mrs Chadra, the Indian diplomat and his wife, who had become involved in the case only because they had been staying in the road for a short while at the time of the murder.

Finally, on the large settee by the heavily-secured windows were Miss Hawkins, and Colonel Templemead-Newson, the inhabitant of the big house on the corner. He was the only survivor of the old families who had lived in the area in the days before it had been overrun by suburbia.

Keane realised that in his injured state, he could not overpower Steet, and that escape was not an option either. For Keane knew who had bought the house and what it was used for. It was now a safe house where a succession of defectors, spies and worse were taken to be debriefed and questioned … and sometimes disposed of.

The various alterations made by the new owners would make it difficult to gain unwanted entry by the police - or anyone else on the outside.

But, as important, it would be even more difficult – impossible really – for anyone on the inside to get out.

Keane wondered how Steet had known this. Was it just the logic of choosing his wife's old home and where she has been killed for his re-trial … or had he somehow known about its new purpose?

Keane also reflected that his own invitation was very cleverly worded with its mention of a reunion of former intelligence colleagues – events that were officially forbidden - but tolerated.

How had Steet known of Keane's past? Steet should have merely known of him as the local CID officer who had conducted the initial investigation. He had been rapidly taken off the case once the powers-that-be in the Met had realised that there were the influential people living in the street and involved in the case.

Keane recalled that they had put that fool Lattice in charge of the investigation - someone who Keane had no respect for. Even at the time, Keane had felt that it had been all-too-easy to pin the murder charge on Steet. From what he had seen, the evidence was at best weak rather then conclusive. But then Lattice would, as usual, have tilted all the evidence he had found to get a quick result and another feather in his cap as one of the Met's top detectives.

Keane was brought back to the present from his recollections by Steet.

"Come on, Inspector, no time for day dreaming - let's get on with the investigation! Pull your chair over to the right hand side of the room so you can see everyone clearly – and I can keep a close eye on you. That's right. And no tricks, please, even if you are tempted to display your rather rusty specialist training.

"You are not mobile enough to get across to me sufficiently quickly to overpower me, and I would hate to shoot the Judge!"

Whatever had happened in the past, it was very clear to Keane that Jim Steet now had them all in his power until he had finished his trial … and his threatened execution.

For Keane was in no doubt that, once Steet had identified the guilty one, he or she would die.

The only question was, would he let the rest of them go free at the end. And that was a question that Keane pondered on as the re-trial commenced.

CHAPTER 2
The shadow of the gallows

Steet's story

The hangman's got a job to do
Just like you and me
It's a thing he does some days
Oh so carefully

He never gets complaints or gripes
Not a sound is heard
And as they drop he always says
They got what they deserved

Jim Steet looked at Mrs Ruane and smiled but without any trace of humour, "You were the one that wanted me hanged. That's not the way to treat your son-in-law."

"You were never our son-in-law, you were just someone we disapproved of who married our daughter. That's completely different. You slithered and slimed your way into her affections, but you never fooled me.

"Then you slithered out of the hangman's noose through all that psychological twaddle of disturbed mind. In my view, anyone who is disturbed enough to murder should be hanged anyway."

Keane interrupted their bad-tempered conversation. "Why were you so against Jim Steet?"

Mrs Ruane looked over to Steet with undisguised venom: "We had it all arranged. Elizabeth was going to marry the son of a good friend of ours – an eminent Judge – and his son was someone who would be a suitable match for our special little girl."

Mr Ruane added, "Yes, Inspector, as my wife says, we had arranged a far more suitable husband. A good boy with prospects, not like that criminal over there."

Steet said to Keane, "They kept talking to her about Tom, the son of their friend Sir Richard. When Lizzie and I had a date, I would find that they'd deliberately booked tickets to the Opera for her to go with them along with Sir Richard and his wife ... and Tom.

"No, they didn't like to see us happy together. I could see the anger in their eyes and ..."

Mrs Ruane interrupted: "She was not meant to be happy with you – that was not possible – she was brought up to be happy with someone of her own class, not someone from the other side of the hill."

Jim Steet waved at her to be quiet and she lapsed into a sulky silence as he continued his story.

"Do you want to tell me your version of what happened that day?" Keane asked.

Jim Steet nodded.

"First, if we accept you did not murder Lizzie, when did you discover the body?"

"I went to pick her up from the house after lunch ..."

"But I seem to remember that you were not allowed in the house?"

"... Not usually, but that day she said her parents would be out and I could come round and then we were going to a film."

"What film was it?"

Mr Ruane interrupted, "what the hell does it matter what the film was!"

Keane looked across at him. "As I am the judge, I will ask the questions. Well?"

Jim Steet looked at Keane almost admiringly, "That's right Inspector, you tell him. He's too fond of his own voice. It was Belle de Jour. I liked Catherine Deneuve and Lizzie teased me about it, but said we could go."

He stopped, suddenly unable to continue – but the gun in his hand remained steady and ready.

"Some unsuitable French ...", began Mr Ruane.

"Will you please be quiet!" said Keane irritated by the pompous little man, with his attempts to be decisive rather undermined by his rather high, squeaky voice.

"Carry on, Jim. Who opened the door?

"No one. It was on the latch. I assumed Lizzie had done that for me, so I walked across the hall into here, and that's when …" He stopped again, but continued after a few seconds.

" … That's when I found her. She was lying there on the sofa. Stretched out and lifeless. I'd never seen a dead body before but I knew straight away she was dead,."

"And then?"

"I ran into out into the hall and into the kitchen."

"Why there?"

I don't know even now. I suppose because the phone was there. But when I went in there those two were sitting like statues. I called to them but they didn't react or move. So I ran out into the street and down to the Colonel's house. I knew that he would know what to do."

The Colonel started to speak, "Seen too many dead bodies in my time …" He stopped seeing Keane's look.

"And then?"

"The Colonel took one look at Lizzie and said, 'nothing we can do, Jim, she's dead.'" Then he left me there with her , and went off to call the police.

"After that it was all like some horrible dream. I just stood there until the police arrived.

"Then you came in, Inspector, and told me you were taking me to the station for questioning.

"They took me out to the car with her mother and father shouting that I'd murdered their daughter and the police trying to calm them and keep them away from me."

Keane recalled the events of that night very well now. When he arrived, Jim was standing quite still by the body and his officers making him move so the photographer could take his pictures and the doctor could make a first inspection.

Then after he had decided to take Steet to the station, there was an unpleasant scene of utmost confusion with the murdered girl's parents haranguing Jim.

After that, Lattice arrived and started to boss Keane and all the local police team in his usual way.

Jim Steet continued. "But I think her parents had already found the body, and then they tricked me into 'discovering' it."

"Why do you say that?" asked Keane.

"As I told you, she was lying there, straight, on the sofa. Wouldn't the deadly poison I am meant to have forced on her have caused her to curl up?"

"Usually, yes. But there was no evidence introduced on that count, as you well know."

"No, the Judge said he did not want to cause distress to her parents, so he accepted the written report of the police doctor who came to the scene."

Keane nodded, "I thought that the position of the body was unusual and mentioned it to the Scotland Yard man who took over from me. But he dismissed my comments. And if I remember correctly, your defending barrister never brought it up."

Steet laughed. "That fool! Did you know he was in the Chambers of Mr Ruane's friend Sir Richard?"

Keane looked across to the Ruane's. "Is that true?'

"No. Complete rubbish. He made that up. Another lie from the murderer."

Frances Hawkins coughed - the sort of cough that means someone has something important to say. "Actually, Inspector, Jim is not lying. I recognised his defence lawyer … I had been introduced to him at the Ruane's … years ago, it's true. But I remember him most clearly. 'meet Brantford – he is in the Chambers of our good friend Sir Richard' - that's what you said, Bill."

Mr Ruane reacted angrily to her statement. "The name is William. I have told you before, Miss Hawkins, don't call me Bill!'

Keane raised his hand to silence Ruane. "Be that as it may, was Jim Steet's defence barrister known to your friend Sir Richard ?"

"None of your damned business! If you want to know, he was appointed by the court's Legal Aid chaps as Steet over there had no money to pay for a Barrister."

Keane shook his head. "But he was linked to you - the victim's parents – who wanted Jim Steet hanged! He should never have been allowed to represent Steet and should have recused himself."

"Beggars can't be choosers, Inspector. Steet was a penniless murderer, he didn't deserve a barrister at all, let alone a top flight one like Brantford, who …"

Steet interrupted, him, saying bitterly. "As far as I was concerned, given the way he represented me, my defence lawyer wanted me convicted as well.

"With a Barrister like that, they didn't need a Prosecutor," he added bitterly.

"What happened at the trial then, Jim," asked Keane. "You believe you did not get a fair trial?"

"The trial was a joke, just that it was serious, not funny. It seemed to me that it was a pre-arranged farce to rubberstamp my conviction.

"There was no attempt to challenge the evidence that was presented. Or to attempt to look at all the facts and the questions that were that were never raised let alone answered – like the position of the body.

"Once the Scotland Yard big shot detective appeared on the scene and took over from you, Inspector, it seemed they were only interested in pleasing Mr and Mrs high-and-mighty over there by getting a conviction for their score book.

"They weren't interested in what I had to say and just kept telling me to confess as they had cast-iron evidence it was me."

Steet looked across at Keane: "Why were you taken off the case after just a few hours? What was that all about?

"You can't read anything sinister into that, Jim. I was just the local CID man on the spot."

Keane ignored Steet's suspicious look. "For a murder like that, Scotland Yard are routinely called in and they take over the investigation. They use the local station it is true, but that is just for convenience. I had nothing further to do with your case."

Keane brought Steet back to the question he had asked a few minutes ago: "So … what happened at the trial?"

"It was all like some horrible nightmare, but I was awake. I sat there as a lot of people came up swore they were telling the truth, then told a bunch of lies."

"Like who?"

"Like those two over there," he pointed at the Ruanes who ignored him the best they could.

"They said we quarrelled all the time and I threatened Lizzie. Gave the court part of a letter she had written saying I was to stop bothering her and not to see her again. Well, I suppose it was in her writing, but she did not write it to me."

He paused. "I wondered then, and still wonder, who she wrote it to. And when she wrote it – maybe to some boyfriend before it got serious with me. Though as I remember, there were no other serious ones."

He was very quiet for a few seconds. "We met at primary school and were always together and started going out when we were teenagers. I promise you Inspector, there were no others that mattered, and she would never have written like that to me."

'Wasn't there a date on it?"

"I don't know, I never saw the letter. Mr Brantford said I couldn't see it as it was privileged evidence that could influence my testimony."

"What a lot of rubbish," interjected Miss Hawkins. "I can tell you Inspector that Brantford was a first class idiot. I know more about the law than him – goodness knows how he ever to got qualify in law at all, let alone become a barrister."

Steet laughed: "Well, as you have heard, he was in chambers of Sir Richard Meaford who was his uncle! Explains a lot, doesn't it."

Mr Ruane looked daggers at Miss Hawkins: "Just because you write second-rate crime novels, doesn't give you the right to insult one of the country's finest barristers with your second-hand knowledge of the law."

This was news to Keane. "What does Mr Ruane mean, Miss Hawkins? From what I remember from my initial involvement with the case, you write for the BBC house magazine."

"Used to, Inspector, but I started writing my crime novels as a pastime and they became so successful that I gave up the day job and now write full-time."

"As Frances Hawkins?"

"Oh, no! Although most of the people here know I write crime novels, they don't know which ones! My writing name is a close secret – only my publisher knows."

There was a pause as Keane and the others waited for her to say more – but she didn't.

She continued, "coming back to the matter in hand, I have to know quite a lot about the law for my books – especially trial procedure - and as Jim says, his trial was a travesty."

Jim nodded in agreement with her and continued: "so as I was saying, it was a waste of time, the Judge seemed to want to get it over with, my barrister wanted me convicted and the witnesses – especially Lizzie's parents – lied through their back teeth saying that we argued all the time.

"Think about it – 'cos I have – a lot. No one asked where I got the poison. No one asked how I persuaded her to drink a glass of poisoned wine when she didn't drink wine."

He paused to think of more examples …"

Keane stopped him. "Did Brantford not query those points? Surely he did?"

"No. His standard response to the Judge was 'Nothing to say, your Honour' like some stupid gramophone record that was stuck in a groove.

"The jury were out for a couple of hours and came back with the guilty verdict and that was it. All over in a day. Not much care taken over getting someone hanged!"

"And afterwards?" asked Keane.

"Afterwards in prison, you mean?' Let me tell you all about what it's like to be in the condemned cell, knowing that you have an appointment with the hangman.

"I was there for three weeks after the trial. Each day was hell. I was in a small cell with two warders with me all the time. They tried not to show it, but they were watching me all the time.

"The routine is that on the night before, the hangman has a look at you through the peephole, checking the measurements and working out his plans for the next morning."

Keane knew what happened as he had been present at a few hangings in his time with Q5, although they had not necessarily followed a trial. Just a quick hearing and off to the gallows.

"What next ?"

"Well the hangman is in the next room – though they are not meant to tell you that, so when the time arrives – normally 8am the next morning, he will pop in, take you next door and top you before you even know what has happened. One of the warders told me it is 15 seconds from when he appears in the door to you being dead. He tried to tell me that was humane - but it isn't if you're not guilty!"

"So what happened," asked Keane.

"The door opened and I fully expected to see the man and his team of two warders - one for each side - and the medical officer who pops down to the bottom of the drop to make sure all is well - or not well - depending on your point of view.

"But, no, it was the Governor and a couple of legal eagles. "You have got a reprieve, Steet," he said. coldly "The Home Secretary has seen fit to let you cheat the gallows."

"Well, Sir," I said. "Seeing as I am innocent, I would

not call it cheating the gallows"

Jim Steet then pointed the gun at Mrs Ruane. "I can remember even now his exact words: 'Well, Steet, you have escaped the gallows, but I can tell you, you're not going to have an easy time so long as you are in my prison.'

"After that everything got blurred and I don't remember much. They said I had a complete nervous breakdown."

"Not surprising with all that you'd gone through," said Keane.

"You are right – I found out later that it was quite usual for that to happen with reprieved prisoners. Anyway, when I was out of the hospital into the main prison, and got my senses back in order, I began to tell my side of the story. Most of the other lifers believed me and … well, they looked after me, if that doesn't sound too strange.

"It's a funny thing, Inspector. Honour among thieves you could say.

"They didn't like the fact that I had been framed. As I said earlier, it upsets their professional pride. They were good to me, taught me how to cope inside and survive prison."

"How did you get out?" asked Keane. "It cannot have been easy …"

"I'm not going to tell you details, Inspector, as you might feel that you have to pass on the information after tonight is all over."

He laughed, but not humorously. "Whoever in this room did it, Inspector, it wasn't you! So you are the only one who is certain to get out of here alive. No, Inspector, I will not tell you.

"Let's just leave it that I got out with two others, and

they were real professionals who had equally professional friends outside to help them.

"Once out, we had somewhere arranged for us to stay where we could hide up and make our various plans for the future.

Tubby Smith, one of my fellow escapees, was inside for forgery. He had some job to do for Sid Silverman, our leader so to speak. Don't know what it was as they were very close on what they were doing.

"But as a side issue, he made me those nice invitations you all got. Very impressive weren't they. And a special one for you, Inspector, inviting you to a reunion of your old comrades."

Keane looked sharply at Steet. "Yes, I was going to ask you about that. How did you know about my previous career in the Met. It is very far from being common knowledge."

Steet smiled a secret smile: "Sid told us about that, he seemed to know a lot of things that weren't common knowledge. He seemed very aware of your … interesting past."

He looked around at the others in the room. "You see, our Inspector wasn't always a humble detective in the local nick. He was part of the Met's …"

"That's enough!" said Keane. "What you know, you know, and that can't be undone. But no one else wants to hear your so-called exposée of my past. So leave the topic alone."

Jim Steet smiled another secret smile, but did as he was told

"So, let's get back to the reason you have got us all here - you want to find out the truth about your wife's death,"

said Keane.

Steet looked grimly at Keane. "No, I don't just want to - I will find out the truth."

He looked at Mrs Ruane. "Do you have some lipstick?"

"What are you on about, you stupid boy."

Steet pointed the gun at her. "I asked a civil question. Do you have any lipstick?"

She shook her head and looked around for support from the others in the room, indicating that she thought Steet had gone mad. But she did as he asked and reached into her handbag and produced a gold lipstick case.

Steet pointed to the large mirror that was part of the ornate marble fireplace surround.

"Did any of you play hangman when you were young?" he asked. "Well, I did, and we are going to play a grown up version now."

He said to Mrs Ruane in a calm but taut voice, "use your lipstick to mark up the twelve dashes for the hangman game and we will see who ends up on the gallows at the end!

"We can start with a 'W' for the Colonel's story. 'W for Warrior,' isn't that right Colonel?"

Templemead-Newsom nodded.

"Put a 'W' on the first dash and you can draw the base line as one of the twelve parts of the gallows."

Mrs Ruane did as she was ordered and went back to her chair to sit down looking like she would happily murder Jim Steet.

CHAPTER 3
The best of friends

Col. Templemead-Newson's story

I have a photograph   It's faded now
Taken when we were young
Then they said you were different
That's when the nightmare begun

The fires crackle and the papers burn
The temple walls came crashing down
Then we knew there was no way back
For us there was no return

The Colonel sat bolt upright in his chair. Unlike the others, he did not seem scared of Steet. Keane guessed that the Colonel had seen more guns than any of the others in the room … maybe even more than he had seen during his time with Q5.

Keane had considered again his chances of disarming Steet, but they were slim. It was a Beretta automatic. Fifteen large calibre bullets in the magazine and quick-firing.

Steet seemed to read his thoughts: "No, Inspector Keane, there is no chance that you could disarm me. Then, as I still wouldn't know who killed Lizzie, I would kill everyone in the room to be certain of killing the murderer." He pulled out a small Colt lady's pistol from his jacket. "Fifteen in the Beretta and eight in this. Enough for all of you."

The Colonel suddenly spoke up, "had a chap like him in my platoon in the trenches when I was a subaltern." He looked dispassionately at Steet. "He was a quiet chap, think he was called Andrews, but my memory is not what it was.

"Yes, he was quiet when he came out to the trenches. OK in a scrap, but a bit squeamish. I had to finish off a Boche that he'd shot and not quite killed." The Colonel's eyes glazed over. "Yes, I remember, he was sick afterwards. Called me a murderer. That's what we're here for I told him. Legal Murder. In peacetime they hang you. In wartime you get a medal."

The Colonel looked at Steet calmly. "Yes, he was called Andrews. Same first name as you, Jim. Corporal Jim Andrews from somewhere in Lancashire. As I said, a quiet chap. Then his best chum got killed.

"You know, in those days they kept all the recruits from the same street together. Idea was that they would support each other. Bloody silly idea, typical of the Generals back in Blighty. All it meant was that if a whole platoon got wiped out in a few seconds by a Boche machine-gunner - and that happened more that anyone said at the time - you had a street full of widows and orphans instead of … well, spreading the deaths around as it were."

"What a cynical old goat you are," sneered Mr Ruane.

"Not cynical, Sir. Realistic.

"Anyway, Andrews, was just like Jim. After his chum got his guts split open in front of him by a German bayonet, he went crazy. Kill, kill, kill. That was Andrews. If he had been able to kill every German on God's earth, I swear he would have done it.

"But the good thing for the Army was that he was carefully, cunningly crazy. Not jumping over the wire like some. No, he plotted and planned his expeditions into the German lines to the nth degree. Off he went most nights like a ghost into the darkness and would come back a few hours later. All he would say was 'Ten, Sir' or 'Six tonight, Sir' or however many he'd killed."

The Colonel nodded to Keane, "Yes, Inspector, I can see that you can handle yourself. Sounds like you have been trained to use a gun. But you won't get far with Jim Steet. He's like Jim Andrews now, crazy but careful.

"Yes, he would kill us all now – I can see it in his eyes. But I know just as surely that he did not kill poor Lizzie, because he would not have killed anyone at that time.

"I could see that at the trial. I knew that as a fact, and told that damnfool of a QC, but he wouldn't listen. Not really fair when your QC - who is meant to be defending you - is convinced you are guilty and lets the Judge and Jury know it.

"Man was hopeless. I've always had a poor opinion of legal eagles, sit at home pontificating about rules of war and suchlike. There ain't no rules when you're in the trenches and the Boche are coming at you in droves. Kill or be killed, that's the rule and no legal stay-at-home can avoid that!"

Keane shook his head, exasperated at the long diversion, "That's all very well, Colonel, but how do you know Steet did not kill his wife?"

The Colonel looked at Keane irritably, "I just told you, Inspector, weren't you listening properly! Jim Steet before the murder was just like my man Andrews before the change. Squeamish. No, Steet would not have killed his wife – or anyone - then. But now he's different.

"Like Andrews he is changed. He will kill us all if he is crossed. Someone killed Lizzie – and it wasn't him – so whoever it was will regret that the hangman never got to practice his calling on Steet."

"Is there a Mrs Templemead-Newson?" Asked Keane with some trepidation, not wanting to start a new steam of reminiscences from the Colonel. He could not remember her from his initial investigation, but maybe she had not been a material witness, or was no longer around.

The Colonel coughed and looked down. "No, Inspector, Lady Newson died some time ago."

He seemed to perk up. "But a grand old age – yes, she had a dashed good innings - born at a time when Britannia ruled the waves, not like these modern times."

"And no children?"

"Not with me. We married during the war – the Great War – not the repeat engagement with the Hun. She was in her forties and I was in my thirties, so no children."

He stood up and walked over to the large fireplace, with Steet's gun trained on him all the time. He turned and faced the others. "You youngsters cannot imagine what it was like then. The press and ordinary people thought it would just a brief encounter – over by Christmas they told us. But professional soldiers like myself knew that was nonsense.

"The Huns were well-prepared – more than we were. I said four years at the time and I was right, give or take a few months."

He stared up at the ceiling and his jaw tightened. "What I did not foresee was the scale of our losses, hundreds, thousands, tens of thousands cut down – in just a few bloody days."

Keane tried to bring him back to the present. "You said no children with you? What did that mean?"

"Oh, she had been married before. When she was young. To that cad Major Newson. Absolute bounder. She was only nineteen … no twenty … they had a boy called Douglas who was killed on the Indian Frontier at the turn of the Century. Hmm, a senseless death at a place called Danzai Pass."

"Just the one child, then?

"Er, no. There was a girl, can't remember her name, born a bit later. But by then she and Newson were about to separate and the girl was quietly, and discreetly, adopted.

"Never found out what happened to her – though we did try. She'd be about your age now, Frances." He pointed to Miss Hawkins. "Shame really, how we lost touch, but that was how it was in those days."

"Of course, there was no chance of a divorce then. Would ruin his career and she would have been shunned by Society. Had to wait until Newson died. Luckily he died young, so she got the title and the estate. That's how she got to buy our grand house next door. Cost a small fortune even then."

Keane had a further try at talking about the present rather than the past: "So, you got on well with Lizzie?"

"Dashed fine girl! Goodness knows how she was sired by that fool Ruane over there with Mrs R as a mother. But you sometimes see it in bloodstock, indifferent mare and poor stallion and you get a winner. Reminds me of a horse I once backed at Newmarket …"

Keane interrupted him: "Another time maybe, Colonel. I was asking about your relationship with Lizzie."

"Of course. Yes, you want to get on with the job in hand like a good policeman, not hear the ramblings of an old soldier.

"Where was I? Oh, yes, I was saying she was a fine girl, always cheerful and happy to listen to my stories. She would come round in the afternoons when she was not working and ask me to tell her about the olden days. She would sit there as I rambled on, and if I stopped, would tell me to continue.

"She came round to keep me company the day before she died, and I was telling her about my final posting - at the end of the replay."

"The replay?" asked Keane curious, despite his wish to get the Colonel back to the murder.

"Yes, the Great War was the first round, then the Germans demanded a replay in 1939. And they lost again! Got obsessed with their idea of ruling the world.

"I was in Germany with the occupying forces at the end of the war trying to put it all back together. Country was a mess – our big bombers and the Yank's even bigger bombers saw to that. Burnt-out and blasted buildings were all you could see wherever you looked in the cities.

"Retribution really – I remember when they burned all the Synagogues when they got into power, so it was only a kind of rough justice that we burned down their cities in return."

The Colonel looked across to Steet. "That was the last time I saw her alive, old boy, sitting attentively listening to my war recollections. She never interrupted me like some others." He glared at Keane.

Steet laughed a rare laugh, "Yes, she had a soft spot for you, Colonel. She used to say you were the only one she felt safe with. Who wasn't trying to seduce her."

The Colonel smiled, wryly. "Good God, Steet, had a few flings with fillies in my youth. But I'm in my eighties now. A gallop with a young gal like Lizzie would probably kill me."

He looked rather slyly at Steet and winked at Keane. "Mind you, what a way to go!"

Keane imagined that the Colonel had been quite a lad in his youth. "And what about the day of the murder, the day Lizzie died? Please tell do me about that …"

"I was in my study reading ... it was a history of the Kabul Campaign in '97 ... but I digress," he added, seeing the look in Keane's eyes.

"There was a knock at the front door. It was Paton's day off."

"Paton?" asked Keane.

"Oh, he's my Butler. Chap's a dishonest rogue, drinks my best Claret and thinks I don't notice. I do, but it is hard to get any servants these days, let alone good ones.

"Aha, I see your look, Inspector. I am digressing again. But when you have lived as long as I have, there is so much history and memory attached to each word that a simple sentence can take a long time."

He paused, and seemed to go back inside himself, back into his treasure trove of memories of long-past days.

"Can we get back to the day she died?"

The Colonel was reminiscing now, oblivious to the situation, and the others in the room.

"Ah, the times we had. The old days, with a full complement of servants to look after us - and a team of gardeners to keep the grounds perfect.

"And in the evenings, there were the dances, with pretty girls dancin' their hearts out ... not like the strange gyrations that they call dancing nowadays."

Keane tried yet again: "And what about the day of the murder, the day Lizzie died?"

"I was telling you, Inspector, before you interrupted. I was in my study reading a history of the Kabul Campaign in '97, when the doorbell rang. No Paton around, so I went to answer it and there was young Steet looking like hell. 'Come quickly, Colonel', he said. Lizzie's been taken ill.

"Well, I don't go anywhere quickly nowadays, but I

followed Jim across the lawn and into the house - this house. And in the dining room - this room to be precise - there was Lizzie lying quite still on the sofa in the corner."

He pointed to the sofa where Mr and Mrs Chadra were sitting. They shifted uncomfortably in their seats.

"I knew at once that she was dead. You can tell - can't you Inspector?"

Keane nodded. He knew what the old Colonel meant all too well.

"Told Jim nothing we could do. Go and call the police, I said."

"And what did he do?"

"Walked like a ghost into the kitchen, then came back and told me the Ruanes were there but not compos mentis. He then just stood there, sheet-white and frozen still like he'd been turned to stone. So I went off and called the police."

"But I don't understand - the Ruanes were in the house, why didn't they call the police?"

"I've told you. You're not listening again. They were quite useless, just sitting in the kitchen like two effigies of human beings. In shock would be the most charitable way to describe them.

"That's why Jim came to me, because the Ruanes were no damned good at all. Like shell shock that we had in the first entanglement with the Germans. Mind you, in the those days they had no truck with shell shock – called them cowards and shot them the next morning at dawn. Yes, I've seen some brave men end up like that and …"

Keane once again brought the Colonel back to the present day. "And when the police came?"

"Oh then, the world and his wife appeared … police, police doctors, ambulance men, a photographer. Place was jammed full of them."

All this time, Jim Steet was listening, watching them all, and saying nothing, just occasionally nodding in agreement at the Colonel's narrative.

"That's it really. After a bit I was sent packing and went back to the house and had a stiff whisky. Needed it, I can tell you. Seeing her like that unsettled me.

"Next thing I knew, they had arrested Steet. And that was all I knew about what happened until the trial"

The Colonel gestured at Keane. "Of course, it was you who came to interview me and get a statement. But I did not get anything sensible out of you. I told you at the time it wasn't Steet, but you arrested him all the same."

"No, Colonel, I was only on the sidelines in the case as the local CID officer. Then the case was taken away from me and handed to Scotland Yard. So the decision to arrest Steet was not mine, it was one of their less able Chief Detective Inspectors. I am just trying to remember his name ..."

Steet interrupted: "It was Lattice. Chief Detective Inspector Toby Lattice. Or Inspector Useless as I called him."

Keane was now starting to remember more about Lattice - a smug, rather slack officer who had been promoted above his ability. Keane then remembered something more ... not long after the case, Lattice had later been quietly given early retirement from the Met for reasons that no one had ever been able to find out.

The Colonel had been uncharacteristically quiet all this time, but sprung into life again.

"I kept telling him it wasn't Steet! But he wouldn't listen. Had made his mind up and wasn't going to change it.

"What with the idiot lawyer fellow, seems to me like Steet was ...what do they say in those awful crime books that Paton reads. Oh, sorry Frances, maybe they are the ones you write?"

He looked across at Miss Hawkins who smiled. "They might or might not have been my books, Colonel. You keep trying to find out my pen name, but I am not rising to the bait."

The Colonel shrugged his shoulders, admitting defeat on this occasion. "Well, be that as it may, the fact is I reckon he was 'stitched up'."

There was a long silence as the last few moments were absorbed by everyone in the room.

Jim Steet was the first to speak. "Yep. Stitched up. That is the word for it. But now I am starting to do a bit of re-stitching to get at the real truth."

The Colonel looked across at Steet. "I know you did not kill her, old boy. Like I said to anyone who would listen at the time - not that anyone took any notice of an old soldier – you were not a poisoner and that was bloody obvious to me. Shame it was not obvious to the police.

"Wish I could work out who did do it. As I keep saying, she was a nice gal and people should not be able to go around poisoning nice gals. Too few in the world."

He looked across at Mrs Ruane, someone he clearly had no time for. "Should have poisoned her mother instead."

A thought occurred to Keane as he tried to recall after a long gap - and for a case he had not been involved in at the time. "Tell me Colonel, do you remember seeing the note that was left by the body?"

"Can't think that I do. Never struck me before, but now you ask me, there was no note when I got there. Funny thing that. No I am sure - the note that they went on about wasn't there at first."

Mrs Ruane spoke up: "I don't think the memory of an old man is something to take much notice of, Inspector.

The note was definitely there because we saw it, when …" she suppressed a sob.

"Even after all this time, it upsets me to think of our little girl lying there on the sofa, murdered."

"With the note in her hand?" asked Keane innocently.

"Yes," she said, half-crying.

"Why do you to go on about the bloody note," grumbled Mr Ruane. "Can't you see how upset she is."

When Keane had been in Q5, a few quiet, seemingly innocuous questions often got more out of prisoners than the toughest 'baton-wielders', as they were called in the unit.

"Which hand was the note in?" he asked, looking rather disinterested in the answer to his own questioning.

"Oh, the left hand."

"As she was lying on her left side, it must have been quite crumpled, I suppose?"

"Oh, yes, it was."

"Oh no it wasn't!" Frances Hawkins spoke up like a character in a pantomime scene. "Jim never got to read it, nor did we. But we saw it didn't we when the prosecuting counsel held it up as Exhibit F."

'So what?" said Mr Ruane.

"It was a plain white sheet with two folds, but not crumpled like it would surely have been in the hand of someone dying of poisoning."

Keane said nothing and waited for one or other of the Ruanes to speak.

Frances Hawkins spoke again, explaining her knowledge of the note. "I attended most of the trial as I was looking for ideas for my books. I quite often go to trials to see what happens in a particular case or to get ideas for using as court background in my books.

"So I was most attentive and near to the prosecutor.

No crumples, just folds."

Keane suppressed a smile as Frances Hawkins turned to Mrs Ruane. "Are sure the note was where you said, dear?"

There was no answer. Just was a long silence as Mrs Ruane sat there, her sobs vanished, unmoved and un-moving.

Keane decided it was time to move on. He turned to Ray Raymond. "Your story next, I think Mr Raymond."

As Raymond got up to go to the mirror, Keane mo-tioned him back to his seat. "And I think we will dispense with your hangman game, Jim. It is a nice idea, I guess, but a distraction to the real purpose of us all being here."

Jim nodded. "OK. As you are the Judge, you can make the rules in your court."

CHAPTER 4
The hands of an Angel

Ray Raymond's story

She looked just like an angel
Was all that he could say
Standing in the sunlight
At the break of day

She looked just like an angel
As far as he could tell
But when the tale was fully told
In fact she'd come from hell

"She had the hands of an angel," said Ray Raymond. "The modelling work she did for one of my shoots was exceptional. She could have gone far in the business.

"A few days before …" he grimaced. "Before it happened. We went into the country for a ride. Not my sort of thing really, I am more of a man-about-town person. But she wanted to ride somewhere and so off we went."

He paused and looked down. "I must say I had hopes …" he looked at Steet. "Sorry, old boy, but she was always a bit flirty with me." He stopped when he saw the look in Steet's eyes – and the gun in his hand.

"Not that I gave her any encouragement, old boy. No, it was just a friendly relationship."

Jilly Raymond did not have a gun, but her looks could have killed just as well.

"I introduced her to my agent, although it was not the usual type of artiste she represented. But she was interested in Lizzie's potential.

"Then she came to the studio to add some hand shots for The Listeners, I saw her real talent ..."

Keane interrupted him. "What are hand shots?"

"Oh, often the main actor or actress might be great on a long shot for a scene, but when you need a close up of, say, them picking up the phone, you find they have awful ugly hands.

"That is when you use get someone like Lizzie to do the hand close ups. It's just the same as using stunt men in action movies, really. And she had the ideal hands for that work, small and perfectly formed."

Keane nodded at this new addition to his store of trivial information that might come in useful again in the future.

"Go on, Mr Raymond. Oh, wait a minute - and what is, or are, the listeners?"

He smiled rather patronisingly at Keane's ignorance. "The Listeners is by far the most popular science fiction series on the BBC! It is about aliens who are listening in the on Earth and its affairs – but whether they are friendly or hostile is the key to the great dramatic tension in the plot.

"And I …" he paused for maximum effect. "… I am the Producer – and have been since the inception of the series."

He smiled even more patronisingly, "we are now on our third series of twelve programmes, and as the characters and storylines develop, I can see us running for a long time."

"It's really just the Archers in a vacuum …the vacuum of outer space," added his wife Jilly acidly.

Ray hit back at once with what was obviously a well-rehearsed taunt. "At least I produce a real show, better then being a mere TV puppeteer."

Keane sat silent during this bickering.

Jilly turned to him, "Inspector Keane, Ray is known at the BBC as the Alien Lothario, always sizing up mere Earthling women to see if they are suited to be his next conquest.

"And Lizzie was marked down on his list as worthy of his attentions. The only problem was that she saw through him.

"Maybe she strung him along a bit, to teach him a lesson, but it was just a game to her, and in the end after using him to launch her modelling career, she refused him."

She smiled at Ray, but it was the smile on the face of the tiger. "Isn't that so, dear. But I don't think he killed poor Lizzie, he's too much of a coward to do such a thing."

Keane decided it was time to call a halt to the infighting. He asked the question he would ask each and every one of them in turn: "And what about the day of the murder, the day Lizzie died?"

Ray was quiet for a moment as he thought of the events of that day. He remembered very clearly the day before when he had taken the rather desirable girl from the sound library out for a bit of a spin in his sports car. It was not very practical, nor was it comfortable for the amorous adventure he had planned in the most convenient quiet country lane. But the car - with its gleaming red paintwork, shining wire wheels and deep bucket seats - was a bit of a chick magnet – a phrase he had heard two musicians using in the canteen, and one that rather appealed to him in its trendiness.

But that was the Monday – the day before the awful

Tuesday when Lizzie died.

"Oh, I was at the Studio all day. Tuesday is always Studio day for us."

"With that dark-haired continuity girl that you were planning as your next conquest." Jilly Raymond did not try to hide the contempt in her voice.

Ray kept silent. He wanted to say that she was wrong, it had not been the continuity girl who had been in the sports car, it was the other girl - whose name he had forgotten.

No! The continuity girl has been another occasion – that was when he had shown her the new sound effects studio. He remembered the key turning silently in the lock and the newly-painted smell of the dark, airless studio with the various props arranged around ... the stairs that led nowhere used for staircase sound effects in The Archers … the door bells used for domestic dramas … and the sofa used for … Yes, he remembered what they had used it for.

Once again he was interrupted by that annoying Inspector asking him: "Mr Raymond, I was asking if you were in the studio all day?"

"Oh, yes. When we are working on an episode, we often work all day and all night." He ignored his wife's sarcastic exclamation.

"Yes, I was there all that Tuesday, and I am sure I could find witnesses to prove that, even though it is now some time ago,"

Keane realised that one thing they all had in common was that they all knew how to hate. He had not seen so much hatred compressed into such a confined space since he had been in Q5. And that was different. There it was professional hatred of the 'other side'. This was worse somehow, because it was purely personal.

"You went to the trial?" asked Keane.

"Yes, I did – if you could call it that," he answered.

"What do you mean?"

"It was more like a courtroom drama with a script about a miscarriage of justice and a title like 'The Hanging of Jim Steet'. And I should know about scriptwriting more than anyone in this room."

"Can you explain your comments - what exactly do you mean?"

Ray didn't seem to hear Keane. Instead he sat there in a dream as he thought back - not to the trial - but to the day of Lizzie's long delayed funeral.

He remembered how his mind had been filled with morbid thoughts. He shuddered as he imagined Lizzie's body being cut and sliced up for the pathologists and bits of her relentlessly scanned under the impersonal gaze of their microscopes as they looked for evidence.

Of what, he wondered. It had been established right at the start that she had been poisoned and it did not seem of much interest to know what the poison was. Although he supposed that they could then trace where Steet had got it and present that as evidence in court. But nothing had been said of that, which was strange.

Surely the fact that she had been killed with poison - whatever type it was - that Steet had bought a few days before, would a key point to establish.

But it had just been stated by the prosecuting Counsel she had died as a result of a poison – unspecified – that Steet had administered, and that was that. The Judge had asked the rather useless defence man if he had any questions for the pathologist - but Jim's Barrister said he had not - and promptly sat down.

There were other things during the trial that Ray also found very strange … disturbing really. It had not seemed a very proper trial. Or a very fair one.

All the evidence had been from the prosecution, showing Steet's unsuitability as a husband due to his quick temper and tendency to boss his wife around.

That did not agree with what Ray had seen of them together, and certainly did not seem sufficient grounds for hanging a man. Indeed, if that were so, a fair proportion of the husbands in Britain would be in the dock and sentenced to be hanged.

And the other evidence was just to confirm the fact that Jim Steet had been seen with Lizzie that day, and all the others hadn't, or were away somewhere else. Given he was her husband, it was hardly surprising that he had seen her.

Also the Judge seemed to be keen to get the whole thing over, as if he had another engagement somewhere else He often seemed irritable at any delay in the smooth running of a train of evidence that would point to a guilty verdict.

Ray remembered several times when, once the prosecutor had finished, the Judge had said, 'well, I do not think there is any dispute over that, so I assume you do not wish to cross-examine the witness.' And the defence barrister just replied 'Quite so, your Honour' - and had sat down once again.

Ray was no expert on trials, but as the producer of a top-rated TV series - and often an on-the-set scriptwriter when there was a problem with the dialogue when shooting - he knew how to spot holes in a plot. And the plot of Steet's trial seemed full of holes.

He had wondered on the day of the funeral as he drove up the hill to the cemetery if he should set down his concerns and write to someone. But who would that person be? And would anyone be interested in the worries of a TV producer when the legal experts had decided that Jim Steet was guilty and must hang for it.

The cemetery was on his left, its entrance framed by the famous wrought iron gates – crafted in Victorian times by the renowned firm of Richards & Wallace. The griffins and other fabulous beasts embedded in it seemed to look at Ray with disdain, as if whispering 'You know something is wrong – you should do something about it.'

As he drove up the long cedar-lined drive he passed little groups of mourners – or more likely inquisitive on-lookers attracted by the notoriety of Lizzie's death and the trial. Ray certainty did no recognise any of them.

He parked outside the Chapel and went inside, shivering a little at its damp and cold atmosphere. He looked for a pew that was suitably anonymous - neither at the back, where people coming in would look at him - nor right at the front, where all could see him. He settled on a central pew where Matthew Parry was already sitting, and nodded at him.

Parry leaned over: "Jilly not here?

"No, it's production day for the show. And Priscilla?"

"No, she hates funerals. She jokes she won't even come to her own."

They both laughed uncomfortably.

Matthew Parry leaned over again and said quietly. Very quietly. "Do you think that there was something … wrong … about the trial? A bit, well, one-sided. Like they used to say in the westerns – we're gonna give you a fair trial, followed by a first class hanging."

"I was thinking the same …"

They were interrupted by the organ starting to play some suitably horrible and dark music.

As Ray looked around he saw the coffin being brought in on the shoulders of the undertaker's men, followed by Mrs Ruane carefully dressed in a suitably black outfit, and after her, Mr Ruane dressed in an equally sombre manner.

All-in-all the whole Lizzie business was a puzzle. But it was one that, despite his various misgivings, in the end he was indifferent to. He had his programme to occupy him and his various romances for relaxation – what else could he need.

His long reverie was broken by Inspector Keane's voice breaking in.

"Mr Raymond! Mr Raymond, please! Did you hear me? Have you anything more to say?

Ray Raymond shook his head.

Keane had initially been puzzled at Ray Raymond's lack of real interest in the murder. Especially, as he had admitted, he had hoped to add Lizzie to his apparently long list of conquests.

But and as watched and listened to Ray, Keane realised that here was a man totally self-absorbed by his own importance – he was a leading TV producer, so all other happenings in the world were subservient to that.

He gave up Ray Raymond as a bad job – for now at least – and turned to Jilly Raymond.

"Mrs Raymond - your story please."

CHAPTER 5
The sound of bitter silence

Jilly Raymond's story

Come to me   Come to me
It's later than you think
The hour has come
The hour has gone
And she is in the pink

Her little smiles
Her giggles too
The way she understands
She knew her power
She had him caught
And held him in her hand

Jilly Raymond sniffed. The kind of sniff that she had picked up in her exclusive Girls' School in her early teens and had not grown out of in her early Forties. It was the kind of sniff that spoke volumes – disdainful, superior, and rather unpleasant. And it was meant to be. It was directed at her husband who winced as if she had physically struck him.

"The worst thing is that, until she realised what a cad you were, you were someone she looked up to. An older man, a successful producer, someone who knew people who could help her career."

She sniffed again. He almost cowered at the sound of it.

"But to you, she was just another conquest, another pretty girl to seduce, then cast aside when you tired of her. Then back to me again."

"Shut up, you bitch!" shouted Steet. "You are talking about my wife. My dead wife. My beautiful wife."

"Oh, maybe I could have murdered her if I had found them together. But I never did. And I couldn't poison someone later in cold blood.

"No, if I wanted to kill one of them, I'd have killed him …" She gave a contemptuous glance at Raymond.

She stopped herself and shrugged her shoulders. "No, Jim, dear, if you are looking for culprits, don't bother with me. I didn't kill her. I actually pitied her for the way Ray treated her."

Keane decided to hear more from Jilly Raymond than her views on her husband's apparently limitless conquests. He changed the tone of the questioning.

"When your husband said you were a puppeteer, what did he mean?"

She cast a further look of contempt at Ray. "I am one of the main producers for BBC Children's Programmes and my most popular show is 'Sand Boy', the most loved puppet on British television."

"The only puppet, because - let's face facts - it's an out-dated format," interjected Ray.

Keane gave him a silencing look. Of course, he now knew who Jilly was … 'Auntie Jilly' who appeared in the afternoon with Sand Boy – billed as 'the naughtiest puppet on the beach'. And despite Ray's scorn, it was a big favourite with small children, and at the mention of its catch phrase 'Who's coming in with the tide?', all the kids in the studio audience – and no doubt at home – would shout 'It's Sand Boy, here he comes.'

Keane found the whole set up a bit creepy and nauseating – but then he was not a bored mother sitting at home on a rainy afternoon in Surbiton trying keep the kids amused while her husband was a commuter train ride away enjoying being 'something in the city'.

However, he guessed that Ray's indiscretions were hardly doing Jilly's career prospects at work any favours.

He looked at her as she continued to bitch at Ray, oblivious to the disapproving looks from the rest of Jim's involuntary Jurors. Her narrow face had a drawn look, and the lines around her lips came from a lifetime of bringing them together in a disapproving grimace.

They were a thin red line, pursed and narrow. Her eyes were equally thin and glinted with venom. The nation's favourite TV aunt was not a nice person.

She continued with her barbed comments about her husband.

"Do you want to know how he tried to seduce Lizzie, Inspector? In the studios there is a room - a special room - one that he alone has the key. You've no doubt heard of the 'casting couch' in Hollywood? Well Ray does one better, he has a casting room where he takes his latest flame."

Keane saw in her remarks a rather dangerous woman. And despite her statement that she would not have killed Lizzie, Keane felt that, unlike Ray, she would have carried out the murder if she had felt justified.

Keane returned to his standard question. "And what about the day of the murder, the day Lizzie died? Tell me about that ..."

"I was also at the Studio ... but not the same one as him. Tuesday is our Studio day too - the day when we rehearse the next week's shows. You see, Inspector, we work a week in advance of how our viewers see us, rehearsing and fine tuning each show ready for the actual transmission"

Ray cut in: "Rehearsing a puppet show for kids. Hardly seems worth it, does it Inspector."

It was Keane's turn to give Ray Raymond an acid look.

"Please let your wife continue, Mr Raymond and do not interrupt."

"Actually, Tuesday is a quiet day here on the street, Inspector. I am at work in the studio, so is Ray. Frances Hawkins is also out as it is her script day. It is Auction Day for John. And it is Matthew Parry's operating day at the hospital."

Ray started to speak, "I thought you told me that on the day Lizzie died, you changed…"

He stopped suddenly, silenced by his wife's most acid look.

"Changed?" asked Keane.

"Oh, yes. I forgot, to say. We changed the music for the show's introduction," she said. "We do that from time to time to keep the show fresh. I remember it was that Tuesday when we made an intro change."

She looked around at the others in the room. "Yes, a Tuesday. She picked a good day to die alone."

There was a further silence before Jim Steet spoke from the corner of the room.

"The point is, Mrs Raymond, she did not die alone, did she? Someone …or more than one person … was there to kill her."

He waved his gun impatiently at Keane. "Carry on Inspector. Don't let this lot distract you from getting at the truth. They are very good at that!"

Keane turned back to Jilly Raymond: "You were there at the trial. Giving evidence?"

"Yes, I wanted to tell the court that I knew all about the girl and what she was like. And how she was just as bad as my husband. Using him to get an introduction to his agent.

"Then, once that happened, and she had got what she wanted, she dropped him like a stone and could hardly bear to speak to him."

Jim Steet clicked off the safety catch of the gun in his hand.

"Careful what you say about Lizzie, Mrs Raymond. I know what you are saying isn't true, but it is annoying me all the same."

"Jim, dear, I am sorry that you are upset. But it is the truth, and denying it does not make it less true. Ray will tell you that it is so."

Ray Raymond just shook his head and pursed his lips, saying nothing at all. Keane could not work out if that meant he agreed with his wife - or that he did not want to say more about his relationship with Lizzie.

"What was the reaction to your revelation at the trial?" asked Keane.

"None at all," Jilly said. "It was all a bit strange. I had been called to be a witness by the defence counsel as – so I assumed – he wanted to show Lizzie was a bit flighty and that fact had prompted Jim's attack. But when I got on the stand I was asked a few vague questions and was told I could go."

"Did the prosecutor or Judge ask you anything?"

"No, and after me they took a break and I was told by the defence man that I could leave the court and go home. And that was it."

"You didn't stay to watch the rest of the trial?

"No it was implied that I had done my part and I was no longer wanted around. So off I went, and the next thing I knew was that Jim had been found guilty and would hang for it.

"That is all I know and all I can say, Inspector."

Keane turned his attention to the aftermath of the trial and the continuation of life in the street.

Maybe Jilly thought that with Lizzie dead, Ray would stop his roaming. But, as she explained, she was wrong.

"You would have thought that after one of his fancies had been murdered he would have stopped his roaming. But no. He just carried on as before.

"But at least he has learned to keep his amorous eyes away from the street and its inhabitants. Too close to home. Not that there is anyone in our part of the street who would have any interest in him, despite what he might believe."

It struck Keane that her taunting her husband in this way carried some buried hint or insult to one of the others in the room, but he could not decipher that for now.

To complete what was a rather sparse and unsatisfactory interview, Keane queried: "What did you mean by 'our part of the street'?"

"The Haskins sold their large house at the end of the street a few years ago and it was bought by some developer who built twenty little boxes in its place.

"They are totally out of keeping with the rest of the street and inhabited by tradespeople … greengrocers, chemists, newsagents and the like. Not our sort of people at all.

"We have nothing to do with them and have removed

the Haskins from our social diary … disgraceful behaviour!"

She could not resist a last dig at Ray: "Ray is on closer terms with the lower hill people than we are, aren't you, Ray. They are a younger set with their trendy wives, not to mention the exotic au pair girls from goodness knows where."

Keane had only been partly listening to her complaints about the Haskins and the new houses. He also ignored further allegations of Ray's wandering - but the mention of the chemists did greatly arouse his interest.

"Was it alleged that the local chemists was the place where the poison came from?"

Jim Steet had been quiet for a long time, but this was clearly something that interested him. "No one found out where the poison came from, Inspector, let alone tried to prove that I had bought it.

"It was just taken as read that I had got it from places unknown, but as I was the murderer, that was not worth investigating."

Keane sighed. It seemed that Lattice had carried out his usual investigation, interested only in circumstantial evidence and not looking behind the obvious.

To Lattice, the husband had argued with his wife, his wife was murdered, and the parents provided proof of their stormy relationship - and there was a note that added to evidence of the husband's guilt.

All Lattice had to do was to present his evidence in a convincing way and Steet was convicted. The verdict avoided scratching below the surface of the lives of some influential people who would only cause him trouble.

Keane could now see that it was a very closed affair, and the intimate secrets of the eleven that had been pushed out of sight at the investigation and trial were now being dragged from them.

Despite his misgivings, Keane could feel himself increasingly drawn into the case and gradually realising that, whoever killed Lizzie Steet, it was certainly not her husband.

Edited Summary of C5 Unit Detective Sergeant Wilshire's report on the night of the siege as filed in C5 archives later.

Once it was known that ex-C5 officer Keane was in a level 2 status siege at Safe House Code HG02, through our routine monitoring of police communications, I was dispatched to monitor the situation and, if necessary, call up a full team. While Keane was no longer an operative, the unit's policy was, and is, to look after its ex-members as a matter of self-interest. They know too much to risk them being kidnapped.

Then it was discovered that, whether by accident or design, POII (Person of intelligence interest) code named 'Trinity' was also in the siege. The incident was immediately upgraded to a level 1 status. Trinity was someone C5 had been instructed by the UK Government to look after at any cost.

Initially, we took the fact of both being there of major significance, but in the end it was found to be truly a coincidence, albeit an unfortunate one.

As I approached the corner of the street I could see
that the local police had closed off access to all
but the residents of the nearest houses.

I was challenged at the street entrance, and showed
my C5 high security clearance card. Upon getting
close, I could see and hear the local man, Chief
Detective Inspector Cummings, briefing his team.

DCI Cummings was planning a hostage rescue effort
despite being inexperienced in such procedures. I went
up to the group and informed them C5 was taking over
the surveillance.

I explained I was a Detective Sergeant from C5.
I further explained that as C5 had an interest in the
hostage situation, I was taking over with joint
authority from C5 control and HOSTCOMM - the Met's
hostage command committee.

I asked the four men Cummings had brought in if
any of them had been in a hostage release scenario or
had any training in such a situation. They all shook
their heads. I then asked if any of then knew what
weapon or weapons Steet had? Negative.

I ordered them all to stay as they could
possibly be of some use at some point. But they were
now under my command. Further, I requested Cummings
to return to his desk as I did not want him on site.

I walked off to the control caravan. In this way
the takeover of the operation by C5 was completed.

CHAPTER 6
A most respectable man

Mr Chadra's story

A respectable man is walking down the street
With his eyes on the girls passing by
They smile   He sighs
Too bad 'cos by his side
Is a girl   Young girl
And she's to be his bride

"Inspector Keane, I must tell you I am a most respectable man, and my wife is also most respectable. We do not like being involved with your British domestic criminal cases."

The Sikh Diplomat and his wife were the only ones who hadn't spoken at all during the time they had been held by Steet. They had simply sat quietly and watched all that had gone on so far with a disapproving look.

"Mr Chadra, do you have anything to add to what we are discovering about the situation in the street at the time of the murder?"

Inspector Keane did not think that either of the Chadras would have much to say about what had happened. Mr Chadra was an Indian Diplomat who had been staying in the street with his wife in a rented house while the High Commission found them somewhere more suitable. They were unlikely to know much, or have seen much, or have any views on the matter.

But he was wrong.

"Inspector, we only lived in this street - stayed here really - for a short time. But even so, we saw that it was a very …" He paused and looked at Mrs Chadra. "… a very unhealthy atmosphere. Not good at all. Not the kind of place we would want to live.

"Please understand, it is not a matter of your country not being good enough for us, there is nothing perfectly wrong with your country - just this particular precise street."

He paused.

Keane brought Mr Chadra back to his question. "What did you mean by an unhealthy atmosphere."

"Oh, intrigues, jealousy, hatred. And infidelity. This is not the way we live our lives. As I totally reiterate to you, I am a most respectable man. A diplomat and do not wish to be involved with all of this British way of life."

He looked around, part sadly and part accusingly. "Look at the envy that drives you all, just a small group of British people, behaving like this."

"As our great guru Pundit Upendra Singh once said: "The envy of each of you for the others will eventually destroy you all."

"Hmmm. Be that as it may," said Keane. "What I need to know from you is did you have much to do with Lizzie Ruane … sorry, Steet?"

"No, not really, we lead a quiet life and most of the time I was at the High Commission offices and my wife was at home.

"All the socialising we needed was at official dinners and suchlike arranged by the High Commission. The Commissioner Dr Mehta is a great man - he was even onetime personal physician to Mahatma Gandhi himself!

"Of course, we saw she Lizzie girl around, but like all young people she was interested in herself and her social life, so did not speak much to an elderly Indian couple as we are."

Mrs Chadra added, "to be totally honest with you Inspector, she was disdainful and had no time for us. But we saw what ..."

Mr Chadra interrupted her. "We saw her busy life without wanting or needing to. Comings and goings. In and out of the various houses in the street. Going in to play piano in the house of Mr Parry over there. Unchaperoned!

"That was not right to us, but the sort of thing that goes unremarked in your strange British Society where girls roam the streets with minimum clothes that are not suitable for your miserable, damp climate - and choose and discard their boyfriends like they choose and discard their clothes as fashions change."

Keane could see that their low opinion of Lizzie was not necessarily something bad about Lizzie as such. As they admitted, theirs were the views of very traditional Indians who did not subscribe to modern British values.

"And what about the day of the murder, the day Lizzie died?" asked Keane. "Tell me about that …"

"Oh we were not around that day. Kindly, Mrs Ruane gave us tickets she did not want to go to the very British Opera sitting on the grass. Most uncomfortable, actually, but an interesting view of British culture."

"Glyndebourne?"

"Yes, that was it. And the opera was very strange, all peculiar music and depressing plot. Not like the one the High Commissioner himself invited us to earlier in the year. That was in a proper indoor opera place and lots of cheerful singing."

Keane set aside his curiosity about the Chadra's opinion of British society musical events and focussed on their absence on the day Lizzie Ruane died.

"So, to be certain, you were not around all day?"

"No, we left early in the morning, attended the Opera, stayed overnight in the resort of Eastbourne, where we were with many retired ex-Colonial people, and got back the next morning to hear about the dreadful news."

"What about the trial. Did you give evidence?'

"We did not go to the trial. At that time we were back home in Delhi on our annual leave from our work at the High Commission. And the police said we were not important witnesses and did not need to be there and could go back to India. Anyway, we had Diplomatic Immunity, so they could not have made us give evidence/"

Mr Chadra looked at his wife yet again. It struck Keane that she was the one who ruled Mr C, and her evidence should be more enlightening.

"The police told you that you could leave the country?" Asked Keane, surprised that any witness would be actually told to leave.

"Ah, well, Inspectorji, not the police man exactly. No, it was the lawyer fellow, Brantford. He said, no need to be around, he said please do head back to India for your holiday, old boy. So we went."

"Do you mean, the defence barrister said you could go? What about the police?

"Oh, he said that would not be a problem and that he would inform them."

Keane shook his head in disbelief. That was not right, not proper procedure.

"And after the trial, once Jim Steet had been convicted?"

"We never came back here. While we away, High Commissioner's ADC found us a nice house in the Northwood Hills. A nice area with nice neighbours, not like here."

He looked around. "This is the first time we have been back to this street. In fact, Inspector, we did not really want to come, but thought we should make a showing before we go back to India for good. Our years stationed here are nearly done and we want to get home."

He looked around at the others in the room. "No, we did not want to come back here and I am sorry we did. One of the people in this room killed that girl as sure as eggs is eggs and it was not us, although maybe we have our thoughts on this matter."

Mrs Chadra stopped him by raising her hand. "Be quiet. It is not our business. It is not our country to interfere."

Keane looked sternly at the two: "But it is your place to say what you know or what you suspect. Tell me what that is."

But both Mr and Mrs Chadra shook their heads, and she pursed her lips in a manner that indicated both a refusal to say more and a strong disapproval of what she knew or suspected.

Keane tried once more with the husband: "Mr Chadra, you do have a duty to say …"

He got no further as the Diplomat interjected angrily and most undiplomatically: "We will say no more, it is the affair of the others in the room. It is not for us to interfere."

He then looked away, refusing to meet Keane's eye any more.

CHAPTER 7
Not how we behave in Delhi

Mrs Chadra's story

I remember summer winds
Blowing off the hills
And the gentle rhythms of the temple's evening hymns

I remember summer bells
Ringing out at noon
And the voices joining gently in an ageless tune

Mrs Chadra was quiet for a time, deciding whether she would maintain her silent disapproval of the situation, the people around her, and the UK in general ... or would speak her mind.

Eventually, she spoke: "This is not how we behave in Delhi," said Mrs Chadra. "You British have lost all morals, living like Mughal Emperors, thinking you are above all laws and rule.

"But it will come to an end soon. All such envy and anger will come to a sticky, sticky end. That is something I know as an iron cast fact.

"I saw the Lizzie girl with him," she pointed at Steet. "They were canoodling like two passion birds. That is not what I was brought up to do ... or even to see. In my home town they would have been separated and the boy flogged. The girl, of course, would have been quite un-marriageable after such a display."

Keane assumed, correctly as it turned out, that Mrs Chadra had an arranged marriage to Mr Chadra and definite views on the topic of marriage. "How can you just let people meet each other and marry without knowing the families?

"I see the girls go out to the clubs and come back with boyfriends who are quite unsuitable."

Keane wanted to see whether Mrs Chadra had ever had much to do with Lizzie. Her views on them 'canoodling' were strange, to say the least, as Jim and Lizzie were a married couple.

"Did you speak much to her? He asked.

"I had no talking or indeed any relationship with the Lizzie girl," said Mrs Chadra. "She was not the kind of person I needed to be in contact with, so I was not talking to her,"

"When you say she and Jim were like two passion birds, is that not usual for a newly married couple?"

"Inspector, they were not properly married. As I told you, it was not for her to go off and marry some boy she had met at a club or ..."

Jim Steet interrupted her angrily: "Mrs Chadra, we had known each other since were children, I did not meet her any club ... and as Inspector Keane has told you, we were married!"

She was not to be put off. "The Lizzie girl did not have her parent's permission and they had a far more suitable boy all arranged. It was not for you or her to interfere with the plans of Mr and Ruane."

Keane put his hand up to stop Steet saying any more, He was interested in how Mrs Chadra - who claimed she had never spoken to Lizzie - knew all this.

"When you say a more suitable match was arranged, how did you know that?"

"Oh, Mrs Ruane explained it all to me, She was humiliated and shunned by her social circle when it was discovered that that her choice of husband for her daughter had been spurned by the two of them running off together."

This time Jim Steet was not to be stopped. "What do you mean running off together! We didn't run anywhere, we got married in the church on the corner just a few hundred yards from here … and all our friends came, and my family. It was just that Lizzie's mother and father refused to come and told all Lizzie's family they forbade them to go!"

"It was not appropriate for Mr Ruane and myself - or our family members - to attend such a function," murmured Mrs Ruane. "I would not want to mix with your friends and would be unlikely to have anything in common with your family members,"

This time Keane stood up – rather unsteadily as his injured leg was hurting a lot. But he wanted to get between Mrs Ruane and Steet as he feared Steet would shoot.

He waved at Steet to calm down, but now Keane was angry as well, and walked across to Mrs Ruane.

"Did you tell a pack of lies to Mrs Chadra? "

She looked away, not answering, a stubborn expression on her face.

Keane looked across the table to Mrs Chadra sitting on the sofa in the corner.

"Seems like you were hoodwinked by a rather misguided woman."

The revelation did not cut any ice with Mrs Chadra. "As far as I am concerned, if the parents forbad the wedding, it was not a wedding, just two rebellious young people behaving badly."

Jim Steet motioned to Keane: "Sit down Inspector before you fall over and damage your leg even more. You see the kind of people we lived amongst – a lying mother and a suspicious neighbour."

Keane decided to move on with his questioning. He

limped back to his Judge's chair and sat down again.

"And what about the day of the murder, the day Lizzie died?" asked Keane. "You were away at the Opera?"

"Yes. Much strange music as Mr Chadra says, and sitting on the cold English grass eating our cold English dinner. What a peculiar nation you British are and no mistake.

"So we were away and knew nothing until we got back and saw the commotion in the street with police and other men here there and everywhere.

"They came to us asking many questions, but we told them we were not here. They even asked us about alibis! Such a cheek. We told them they could ask the High Commissioner himself and he would give us an alibi."

She looked at Keane narrowly. "Were you one of the policemen that bothered us? I don't remember you, but all policemen look alike to me. Next thing is, I said to Mr Chadra, they will take us down into small room and try to beat a confession out of us like the police in Delhi do with known goondas."

Keane stopped her outburst. "Mrs, Chadra, we do not do that in Britain - and why on earth would the police think that you had anything to do with Lizzie's death?

Mrs Chadra was not to be reassured. "I know how it works even here – and where did you think our Indian police got their beat and confess ideas from? Yes, it was you British who set up our police and all those other government desk-wallas sitting in their offices bothering honest citizens. All this came from you!"

She was now thoroughly warmed up to her theme. "You see, Mr Inspector, The police like their results and to please the high-up influential people. So a couple of Indian culprits would fit the case most well. All these people," - she waved her hands around the room – "are influencers, yes, top class people."

Keane reflected for a moment that, while the beatings part was not ridiculous, her analysis just about summed up what Lattice had done. He had chosen the least important suspect – one that would give him no trouble – and set out to prove he was the murderer. And in doing so had ignored some obvious facts that did not fit his theory.

Keane returned to Mrs Chadra's accusations: "but the police did not lock you up or beat you, they arrested a British man, Jim Steet, and he was sentenced by a British court to be hanged for the murder. So that really dismisses your ideas."

She was not to be deflected from her theories.

"OK then, nearly as good. Arrest a local boy instead. Perfect for the confession and hanging matter."

She looked across the room at Steet who had watched and listened to all this quietly.

"But he did not kill her. Too stupid I would say. Finding poison and making her take it. Not likely to me, but your police did not think that. They had a good suspect, so case closed and off to the pub, with no beatings necessary. "

Keane was beginning to tire of Mrs Chadra and her prejudices and theories: "You certainly did not kill her, and do not think Jim Steet did, do you have a theory of who did do it?"

Mrs Chadra pursed her lips once more and crossed her arms in a gesture of finality. While Mr Chadra was clearly a highly educated man, and unlikely to say anything he had not fully weighed up and planned, Mrs

Chadra was a plain-spoken woman who spoke her mind. Maybe she did know something, but getting her to say what she knew or suspected would be very difficult.

"I have had my say, Mr Inspector Keane. You are the policeman. It is your job to put finger on collar of killer and take them off to the prison cells. Not my job."

Keane tried another tack with her. "And you were away for the trial.

"Yes, sneakily sent away so we could not give evidence!"

Why do you say that?"

"The lawyer man, Brantford, told us to go, and Mr Chadra obeyed him. But I knew something was up – that sneaky dog legal man had some motive for wanting us out of the country."

What was that," Keane asked, holding his hand up for silence as Mrs Ruane started to say something.

"I do not know specifics, Inspector, but a number of people here were more … friendly … than is proper with the Lizzie girl."

"Go on", said Keane. But before she could continue, there was an angry outburst from Jim Steet.

"What are you getting at, you Indian witch. You never even knew Lizzie and were always giving here nasty looks whenever you met her. Just because she married someone she wanted, not some boy that her parents had arranged, like in your country, it doesn't mean she was bad."

Mrs Chadra stiffened and said angrily, "If she had married the boy her parents chose, instead of someone unsuitable and unofficially chosen like you, she would be here now."

Mrs Ruane smiled and nodded in approval at Mrs Chadra's statement, while Jim Steet started shouting at her.

Keane banged on the table in frustration and said to Steet. "You tricked me here to find out who really killed you wife. Please shut up and let me do it."

Steet lowered the gun a little … but not a lot … it was still ready to shoot. "Carry on Inspector."

"Mrs Chadra, what 'goings on' did you see?"

She stood up and pointed round the room as she spoke. "Mr Raymond was always trying to entice her to his place so she could join the others we heard about."

"How did you know about the others?"

"Oh, from his wife, Mrs Jilly. She was always telling all who would hear about his conquests as she called them. With the kanjaris as we call them back home in in India.

"Then there was Mr Parry – although in India if you are a properly qualified medical men – it is 'Doctor' not just plain Mister."

"Surgeons and Consultants are called 'Mister' in England," Matthew Parry murmured.

"No matter, Doctors, Misters and all other gentlemen do not entertain young unmarried women in their house alone."

Matthew Parry shook his head in rejection. "She came to play the piano, Mrs Chadra."

Nothing daunted, she replied, "You see, he admits it, Inspector. Much music and also no doubt dancing too. Disgraceful."

She continued to point at each of them in turn.

"And all the others were just as bad. The writer lady, who writes unsuitable books, was always taking tea with her - no doubt hearing about the bad people the Lizzie girl met at her work so she can write about them in the books..

"Then there was the Antiques man showing her his treasures and taking her to Auctions in lonely parts of the country where goodness knows what could have happened.

"And even the old Military man's eyes used to light up when she walked past in her short skirt that barely covered her knees and a shirt that did not have enough buttons to be done up fully to her neck as it should have been."

Keane began to understand why, however improper he had been, Brantford had good reason to pack Mrs Chadra and her husband back to India. Although her accusations were way over the top in the carefree modern atmosphere of the 60s, her evidence would have caused a sensation in the press and painted Lizzie as some kind of playgirl who, as the gutter press were always keen to say, got what she deserved.

Keane wondered why on earth they had come to England given the low opinion they had of most English people and of the English way of life.

"Why did you come here in first place – I'm sure you can choose where you are posted?"

She laughed: "Inspector, I go where my husband takes me, and he goes where his Government tells him. It is as simple as that. We are not part of the loose-living easygoing culture that has taken over in this country."

Keane had one last try to get some result from his questioning of the reactionary couple.

"So, Mrs Chadra, you hinted earlier that you and Mr Chadra knew who killed her? Of course, it is my job to prove that, but maybe you can give me a clue."

"Inspector, it was all of them!"

He looked puzzled. Surely even this rather obsessed woman did not mean a gang-style mass killing!

"When you say – all of them – what do you mean?"

She shook her head in annoyance at Keane's stupidity, "Any of them - and all of them - could have done it. That's what I mean. You just have to find out which particular one did it."

Keane gave up on her – for now at least.

He looked at his watch, it was nearly midnight and no nearer the truth.

"Mr Thorpe, please your story."

CHAPTER 8
Priceless

Tristan Thorpe's story

Try as he might, he couldn't forget
Those nights of long ago
When first he won, but then he lost
That precious fragile girl

And time flies by, days came and go
Like cruel cascading sands
He counts the days, since she walked away
As she waved her goodbye hands

Tristan Thorpe looked thoughtful and said nothing for a while. And Steet pointed the gun threateningly at him. "Silence can mean guilt. Have your say or I will assume you have something to hide."

When Tristan Thorpe did speak at last, it seemed totally irrelevant: "In the course of my career I have to value things. Of course, some are easy … when someone brings a Picasso to value I can set that against other works of his from the same period, of its artistic merits, its provenance - and even its size ..."

He laughed as the others stared at him. He misunderstood their surprise.

"Oh, yes, for big businesses wanting art for the boardroom, it is the size that matters. Ten square foot of a very minor French impressionist is of far more value to them than a few square inches of a Da Vinci …"

Steet interrupted him," what the hell is that do with Lizzie's death!"

"Oh, priceless. That's what I am trying to tell you. She was like a priceless work of art. And you, Jim, didn't appreciate that."

Keane raised his hand to silence them both. "Please, Mr Thorpe, tell us what you knew about Lizzie - and what relationship you had with her."

"I knew her when she was young, when she was the pretty little girl in the kindergarten at the top of the hill, and she was there with Jim and me. Three little kids growing up together. As she got older, she seemed to attract the boys like a moth to a flame, but she only had eyes for Jim."

Keane looked carefully at Thorpe. "So, you never ..." He left the words unsaid.

"Just once, Inspector. Jim was away and they'd had one of their arguments."

Thorpe looked across at Steet, obviously worried that there would be an explosion of anger. But Jim Steet sat watching, never relaxing his surveillance of everyone in the room.

"We went out to a party and, for that one crazy night, danced and romanced until dawn."

He shook his head sadly. "Then it was like it had never happened and she was back with Jim. After that we were back to being friends - as much as anyone was her friend."

"What do you mean by that?" asked Keane.

"Oh, she was popular, like I said. But there was always a part of her that was secret ... private, that no one could get at."

"Of course, I saw her around because, like me, she lived on the street, but we moved in different circles and I was away so much on my buying trips.

"Then I saw her at an auction where I had gone to buy a particularly good watercolour by J.T. McGraw – an excellent 1920s artist who is little-known nowadays.

"She was there with someone who was bidding for a horrible piece of post war kitsch …"

Who was it?" asked Keane

"I don't know Inspector. She didn't introduce me, just came over and asked how I was. Asked me if I was happy and why was I there.

"I said I'd be happier if I was there with her. She just laughed, touched my sleeve gently and said 'no one can be truly happy, you know.' Then she walked back to her companion and they left."

He gave a sad smile at the memory and added, "I hardly saw her after that, maybe a few times as she walked down the street and I was passing on the other side."

"Did you see her at all in those last few days before she died?'

"Yes, Inspector." Thorpe looked across at Steet who was looking directly at him.

"The last time I saw her it was like a cry for help – or more for an escape. She called me up, really out of the blue, as we had not seen each other for a while. She asked me if I would take her to the coast for a day to get away from this lot ..."

He waved his hands around the room.

"So we drove down to the seaside and chatted about when we were young …"

He paused and looked sad. "For a few hours it was like we were together as a couple. She told me that she'd had enough of the street and its inbred atmosphere. She said she was planning to go a long way from here where no one could bother her."

"Where?" asked Keane.

"She didn't say, she just seemed like she'd had enough. We walked along the front, went to the Odeon and saw a film, talked some more and had some dinner, then set off home.

" I hoped that … well, I don't really know what I hoped, to be frank. It was all like a dream. And seems even more like that now - after what happened.

"As we drove out on the road from the seaside, she suddenly said to me, 'I have changed my mind about running away. And I know what you have been thinking, but it can never work between us. We both know that. Take me home.'

"So, we drove back in silence and she got out at the end of the street so no one would see us together – and that was it."

He was silent again. Keane could see that Tristan Thorpe was a man of silences.

"And what about the day of the murder, the day Lizzie died?" asked Keane. "Tell me about that …"

"I was not here when … it … happened. You see Tuesday is my main Auction day. I pick an interesting one anywhere in the country and go to buy what fits my tastes or – if I have a commission – what my client is after.

"I remember that day well. I had to go out to the stately home of an old-established family that had - to be frank - fallen on hard times.

"It was a most successful day. I bought a unique olyphant …"

Keane interrupted, "An elephant?"

"No Inspector, an olyphant." He emphasised the pronunciation carefully.

"Oh, I thought you meant a stuffed elephant from the days of the Raj, like you get tigers and so on."

Thorpe laughed. "Oh, yes, I see the confusion."

"An 'olyphant' is a hunting or battle horn, made of ivory. This one was very old. I guessed 14th Century, and was in a job lot of scrimshaw …"

This time it was Matthew Parry who interrupted him. "I thought scrimshaw was whale bone carving?"

"Yes, most often, but in the trade we use it for all carved objects in whale bone, walrus bone – and ivory."

"Where was the auction?" asked Miss Hawkins." We usually never hear the end of it if you do well and end up with a treasure you got for a song. We never heard you talk about this one."

"Can't tell you, Frances. Even though it was some time ago. It was a well-known hard-up family, and these private auctions are always terribly discreet as they do not want anyone to know their circumstances.

"And they are often very productive for specialists like me as the mainstream dealers go for the big items – such as the missing Van Gogh that has hung in the gallery for decades.

"But I know it is the job lots that often contain the really valuable items for me. Ones that are jumbled together and go for a few hundred guineas. I just need to find one thing of real value and I have paid the rent for a few months."

"How much did you buy and sell your olyphant for?" asked Keane intrigued, despite wanting to get on.

"I seem to remember I paid two hun-

dred guineas for the lot and sold the olyphant for …
well, I will tell you … one hundred thousand guineas to a
museum somewhere in Europe.

"Good lord," said Matthew. "That would pay for the
rent for more then a few months.!"

"I have expenses to cover and commission to pay –
and to pay for the weeks and weeks where I do not get
anything worthwhile," Thorpe said defensively.

There was a silence in the room, ended by the Colonel
piping up. "Had a chap named Scrimshaw in my Regiment now I come to think of it. I suppose his father must
have been a whaler. Or an ivory trader. Or an ..."

"I would like us to get back to the day she died, if you
don't mind," said Keane hastily stopping a likely flow of
more reminiscences

"It seems to me that it must have been a very quiet
and silent street the day she died," mused Keane. "Everyone was somewhere else."

"Yes, I rather wondered about that, at the time" said
Thorpe. "As Ray said, it is his day at the TV Centre also
for Jilly. Frances was there as well. Then I was at the auction, and Matthew was at the Hospital. Those who would
have been around, like the Chadra's were off in Sussex,
enjoying the opera."

He gave an amused look at Mr Chadra who grimaced
at the memory of their day of English culture. "While the
Colonel was at a Regimental reunion as I remember."

The Colonel nodded, "21st Suffolks, the 'Up-and-
Get-Em' boys. Last Regiment I was with. Damn fine lot
and even though most of the men I knew are now dead,
decrepit or gaga. But the ones that are compos mentis are

still up for a good night out."

Keane feared yet another long string of memories about past times from the Colonel, so he changed the subject and moved on to the trial.

"What about the trial? What did you make of the proceedings there?"

"I did not go, Inspector. I was not called to give evidence and I could not face going."

He smiled sadly. "Of course, I heard that Jim had been convicted, but somehow I did not think he had done it. That he could do such a thing.

"Maybe he could lose his temper and strike out wildly. Maybe. But to go and buy poison to kill Lizzie and then administer it. No, that seemed out of character. And they never found out where he got it from, did they?"

Keane nodded in agreement, "No, it was just taken as read that he had obtained it and that was it. A good Counsel would he picked up on that point, but it seems his didn't"

Steet said: "You're too right Inspector. Brantford said it did not matter as I could have got hold of it anywhere, so the exact place was not important."

Keane looked at him amazed. "Not important that there was no link with you and the poison that killed her? And what about how you persuaded her to take it?"

"They said I had forced her to take it, but that would not be raised in court as it would be too distressing for her parents."

Keane shook his head in disbelief. He looked at Mrs Ruane and said pointedly to Steet: "being hanged as a result of a conviction at such an improperly conducted trial was no doubt distressing for you."

Mrs Ruane started up again. "Inspector, the Judge was doing his job, sparing our feelings in omitting the horrible details when we all knew he killed her and just needed to get the trial over and done with, and get that monster hanged."

"Mrs Ruane, I tell you again, please keep quiet. You will get your turn to speak."

He looked at Tristan Thorpe. "Anything else you want to add, Mr Thorpe?"

"Not from the trial, as I said, I was not there. Jim was found guilty and that was the end of it.

"Actually, I have been away in New York a lot over the last couple of years working on a commission from a wealthy American to locate some rare Renaissance paintings, so I did not know all the news. I had assumed Steet had been hanged. No one told me about the reprieve."

Mrs Ruane made a sound as if to speak, but Keane gave her a severe glance and she thought better of it.

Tristan Thorpe continued so quietly that they could hardly hear him. "I often think of her. How she was when she was growing up and we were all young. It was not like she became."

"And what was that?"

"Oh, a bit of a ..." he paused conscious of Steet's unwavering gun. "No, Jim, I am not going to say anything bad of her." He paused some more and thought for a few seconds before choosing his words carefully. "She became a bit of a ... lost soul, I would say.

"She had her modelling work, but I always thought that was almost insulting - that people only wanted to see her hands. Not her face or the rest of her.

"Also, I do not think she liked the kind of people she had to work with – photographers and agents and a host of hangers on. Not the kind of people she was used to.

"Yes, she was a lost soul who never found happiness. That's it Inspector. That is all I have to say."

There was a long silence in the room, broken by Jim Steet. "Carry on Inspector. I would guess your police chums are also planning how to break in and free every-one." He looked across at his group of involuntary jurors.

"But it would not do them any good, because this is a well-secured house, and by the time they finished break-ing down the doors or the shuttered windows, I would have put a bullet into each and every one of you. Which would be a pity because only one of you deserves to die."

Mrs Ruane shouted at him. "You don't scare me. You are the killer, we all know that, you just want an excuse to kill someone to satisfy your blood lust."

She started to get up, but Keane waved her down. "That is not the case. If he wanted to kill for the sake of it, he could simply do it now - isn't that right, Jim?"

"Yes, Inspector. What I want is the truth. So continue your interrogations, please. I am finding all this very revealing. You are confirming the layers of relationships and emotions that exist in the street."

The un-shut-up-able Mrs Ruane couldn't help adding, "that's because you were an outsider, from the ordinary houses in that road on the other side of the hill. How could you know how people like us live. We are in a dif-ferent class to you."

Kean ignored her.

"Mr Parry, you are next …" he turned to the rather suave and elegant Surgeon who was sitting next to – but not close to – his wife.

CHAPTER 9
A stranger in the house

Matthew Parry's story

Notes hang in the empty air
The piano lid falls shut
She played just like an Angel
And wants to love him … but

She wants the guy with eyes so blue
A head that turns away
She asks if she could love him true
But his cold arms push her away

"Of course, I am good at looking at people dispassionately. That's my job," said Matthew Parry. He'd walked over to the small drinks table next to the fireplace and helped himself to the ruby red wine in a cut glass decanter that sat there along with a selection of bottles ready for the guests.

Mr Ruane stared at him in disapproval as if the wine being poured was still his and not something chargeable to the Government's hospitality budget. But Parry didn't notice him, or more likely did not care to.

"A surgeon sees people in a way that no one else does. Maybe that was why I could see the value of Lizzie to you all. You all desired her - but she did not need any of you."

Priscilla Parry laughed sarcastically, "Well, she certainly did not desire you."

"On the contrary, dear girl, she did. She propositioned me twice. But you are right in a way, in that it was not a mutual desire."

Priscilla Parry addressed the whole room as if she was

in one of the TV dramas Ray Raymond produced. "You see, my husband is what I believe the younger set call gay. Queer. A homosexual. Not at all interested in women."

Parry said nothing, and there was a silence broken by Steet who said sarcastically: "Well, that is one person who I can be certain did not sleep with my wife."

Matthew Parry continued, ignoring both his wife and Steet: "She used to come round now and then when Priscilla was away. She would play the piano for me. We have a fine Steinway that Priscilla's parents gave us as a wedding present. It is really wasted on us, but she was a really good pianist and didn't have a piano at home. So she appreciated the chance to play."

He glanced across the room to Steet. "She played just like an angel and could have been a professional pianist I would say, had she wanted. But she just enjoyed playing – not for me – but for herself."

He paused and took another sip of the wine. "She would come play all sorts of tunes. Some I knew, others she told me she had made up. The sound of her playing echoed round the empty house as I was the only one there most of the time."

Mrs Parry laughed, but not in amusement. "Why should I want to hang around while you read your medical books on how to operate without killing too many patients and play music – or listen to that stupid girl bash away on our lovely piano."

She looked around for support, but got none.

The Colonel said, "don't agree Priscilla, thought she was a dab hand at the piano myself. She used to play marches for me sometimes – Chopin, I think?"

Matthew Parry smiled, "yes, Chopin wrote some excellent march music and she played that for me as well.

"Then, she stopped coming."

"Why?"

Priscilla cut in, "because she saw one of his 'friends', that's why!"

She stopped when Keane looked angrily at her.

Matthew Parry continued: "One day, a few weeks before she died, she came round unexpectedly to play. I had given her a key so she could let herself in when she wanted if we were away ..."

"You did what!" exclaimed Priscilla Parry. "You never told me."

"Well that is what I did, and it was nothing to you. Anyway, that day I had my friend to stay the night before. Priscilla was away, as she often is.

"He came down to see who was playing as he knew I couldn't play like that."

Matthew Parry took another sip of the wine. "Excellent wine, Bill! A Chateaux Marguax, of course. A '57 if I am not mistaken. Those Government guests are well looked after aren't they! Better wine than when you were here."

"You should bloody well know as you are drinking it. And I still care as it still goes on my tax bill, and this is not the time for a drinking session," Mr Ruane snarled at Matthew Parry. "And do not call me Bill, my name is William. I don't bloody well call you Matt!"

Parry smiled, enjoying taunting Mr Ruane almost as much as he was enjoying the wine. "Oh, call me Matt. I don't mind - Bill!"

He looked closely around the room and turned to Keane. "So what is this place now? We hear it is some kind of Government guest house. For what ..."

Frances Hawkins said disapprovingly: "I think you mean 'for whom', Matthew."

He laughed, "You are right, Frances, I was always better at biology that English grammar at school."

"That is good news for the patients under your knife!"

Matthew Parry was about to continue when Keane stopped them.

"Miss Hawkins and Mr Parry, please can we get back to the matter in hand."

"Of course, Apologies Inspector. So, she saw my friend and stopped playing. I suppose it was obvious what the situation was. She slammed the piano lid shut and, without saying a word, walked off into the hall and out of the front door, slamming that shut too."

He looked down at the floor. "I saw her a few times after that, but she would not speak to me, just turned her back on me."

"That must have been hard for you?" said Keane.

Matthew Parry shrugged his shoulders," I am used to it, Inspector. But, yes, it was hard coming from someone I liked and had watched grow up."

Frances Hawkins butted in, "she always had a bit of a thing for you, Matthew. Ever since she was a teenager. So finding out you were not interested in her - or indeed in any women - would have hit her hard."

"I never knew that."

Frances Hawkins laughed, "well, perhaps as a woman I saw it more clearly than you did. But I suppose you wouldn't have noticed the girl's all-too-obvious interest in you!"

Parry looked at Miss Hawkins, surprised: "no, young girls being interested in me was not something I noticed."

Jilly Raymond came to life. "Unlike that husband of mine. We always knew of your situation and just respected it, Matthew."

She turned to Priscilla. "You should be glad that Matthew could be trusted in a roomful of young, attractive nurses. Ray gets excited even when he drives past a hospital!"

"And what about the day of the murder, the day Lizzie died?" asked Keane. "Tell me about that …"

"Not much to tell. It was a Tuesday and that is my main operating day at the hospital. I usually spend Monday looking at the case notes and maybe technical papers in one of the relevant medical journals. Then Tuesday is a busy day."

He looked at Keane, inquiringly. "Do really you want to know all this?"

"Yes, or at least the outline. Not every cut as it were."

Parry smiled thinly. "Well, I get up late, go the hospital around midday, have one or two hours preparing, planning with colleagues ... the anaesthetist and so on. Then the patient is prepared and I 'go into action', as you policemen would say, in the late afternoon. And the next few hours is when I earn my keep!"

"How long will an operation take?

"Oh, about six or seven hours. It does depend of the exact state of the patient – and of the donor heart. I'd normally finish my star turn, as it were, around nine in the evening and if all has gone well leave it to one of the less … eminent surgeons who has been assisting to do the tidying up and sewing up."

So you only do one operation a day."

"Good lord, Inspector, it's not a production line! If a patient gets under my care, they are at the end of the road in terms of what can be done for them. I do one operation each week and I can assure you that is enough for me. I then need the rest of the week to recover."

"So you were out on that fateful Tuesday from, let us say, noon to ten at night?"

"Precisely. By the time I got back home, the initial hoo-hah must have been over and I really did not notice anything.

"The Ruane's house is screened from ours by the trees, so we cannot really see down their drive. I was so exhausted I went straight to bed and it was only the next morning when Frances telephoned me that I found out what had happened."

"Mrs Parry was away, then?" asked Keane.

Matthew Parry started to answer, but she interrupted.

"I was speaking at an important event for a charity I am deeply involved with – it was in Harrogate – that's in Yorkshire I think. I am not really good on the exact geography of all those provincial towns. I remember it was very cold and the food in the hotel was disgusting. My keynote speech was …"

"Thank you, Mrs Parry, we will come to your story very soon.

Matthew Parry was now seated and looked around. "Not that much has changed since the new tenants moved in. Looks to me like the same dated furniture – or very similar. Even the carpet looks the similar."

He looked again at Keane: You didn't get round to telling us for whom," he glanced at Miss Hawkins, " this is now used for."

Keane nodded in agreement. "You are right I didn't."

Without giving Parry time to respond, Keane re-started his questioning. "And once all the so-called excitement was over, Jim Steet had been arrested and the trial was about to get under way – did you have any involvement with the trial?"

"I was asked to give evidence about Lizzie's state of mind – how unhappy she'd been and so on. But in the end I did not."

Mrs Parry added, "we did not want to be involved in going to a sordid murder case – not our sort of occasion.

"The policeman tried to make Matthew go, but I had a quiet word with a couple of rather senior people I know well in the legal profession. And they had words with others down the line and they very much got the message that we would not want to be called."

Keane looked at her and then at Matthew Parry who shook his head as if to say that was all that would be said on the matter of the trial.

"And afterwards?"

Mrs Parry again spoke for him. "What do you mean 'afterwards'. There was no afterwards. We got on with our lives and hoped the scandal of having a murderer in our midst would soon be forgotten by the press.

Matthew Parry added, "we sold the piano."

"Sold it? Why?"

Mrs Parry looked at Keane in astonishment. "Are all policemen stupid? Of course we sold it. I was not having a pianoforte played by a murder victim in my house.

"I offered it to one of the London concert halls as a practice piano – I am one of their trustees. But they didn't want it so Tristan got one of his auctioneer friends to dispose of it."

Tristan Thorpe looked pained. "Priscilla, it was not merely disposed of – it was a very fine and very early 1890s Steinway that was sold for a substantial sum at a Sotheby's antique musical instrument auction."

"Well, we were well rid of it, that is all I can say."

Keane suspected that was not all she could or would say. "So, Mrs Parry, can we hear your comments on what happened."

CHAPTER 10
Such a scandal

Mrs Parry's story

Across the crowded room
Your roaming eyes met his
He held you far too close
As they played a waltz by Liszt

In the silent sinful night
You sneaked across the lawn
Hidden far from prying eyes
You strayed until the dawn

It was quite a scandal," said Mrs Parry. "Really it was nothing to do with us and yet it affected the house values in the street very badly."

She looked at Steet. "We were planning to move and had to delay it, her death was really most inconvenient on all fronts."

She turned to her husband. "Do you remember what those ghastly papers said 'Murder comes to Rotten Row'. What a nerve, those reporters, like jackals round a corpse.

"We could not get rid of them, bribing the man at the gate to get through, then knocking on our door, asking if we knew the dead girl. When I was back home in Worcestershire, where I grew up, we had a lodge at the end of the drive and they would not have got near the house.

"Can you believe it - when I asked the policemen - who were wandering around with nothing much to do as far as I could see - to arrest the reporters for trespass, they did not seem at all interested in my complaint."

Keane suppressed a laugh. He imagined the scene of the busy crime officers being accosted by Mrs Parry.

In Priscilla Parry's eyes, she had come down in the world. To many, even to most, being the wife of one of the country's top surgeons would be a sign of a certain social standing. They certainly had more money than all the others in the room added together.

But that was not where she had come from. To her, they were trapped in a suburban street, with people in trade or commerce as neighbours.

She had been brought up in her family's place in the country where her father was the local squire and her mother was a leading socialite. Like Pricilla, her mother too believed she had married beneath her - she was rumoured to be daughter of the one of the leading noble families of the kingdom.

"Did you get on with Lizzie?" Keane asked.

"What on earth do you mean by 'get on'? Why should I have anything to do with a rather dysfunctional girl who happened to live opposite. And if I had got my way, we would not have been living near here in any case.

"No, other than feeling very sorry for poor William …" she stopped and corrected herself. "Mr Ruane, and - of course - Mrs Ruane," she added hurriedly.

Much too hurriedly, Keane thought. He wondered if, in the convoluted set of relationships between the residents of the street, there had been anything between Mrs Parry and Mr Ruane. It seemed most unlikely, as Keane imagined Mrs Parry would not deign to have an affair with anyone less than a knight of the Realm. But he had seen far more unlikely liaisons in his time.

" …apart from feeling sorry for Mr and Mrs Ruane, I had nothing to do with Miss Ruane, nor did I want or need to. I do not like children or any age or – as I believe we must now call them – young adults."

"You do not have any children?" asked Keane

She did not answer, but her look of horror at the thought was enough for Keane to move on.

"And what about the day of the murder, the day Lizzie died?" asked Keane. "Tell me about that …"

"I have already told you, Inspector, I was in Harrogate. Don't you listen to people when they tell you things. You can't be a very good policeman if you don't listen properly."

Steet laughed. "There you are Inspector, that's telling you. No wonder you got taken off the case!"

Keane said: "No, that was not the situation. It was a level 2 murder case and they are always taken away from local CID officers and handed to the murder squad."

"You sound a bit defensive about it," said Steet who was obviously enjoying Keane's discomfort.

Keane wanted to find out more about how Priscilla Parry spent her time when she was not at home – presumably she was ruling it over another set of people.

"You are obviously well-connected, and very worthily devote much for your time to charitable matters. Are you involved with any in this area?"

"Oh, yes, Inspector, this is a very historic place and I am pleased to be the Patron of the local Society."

"What society is that?"

Matthew Parry and Tristan Thorpe both laughed together at Keane's major gaffe.

"Inspector Keane, it is simply the Society. That is its name and anyone round here would know that. We do not need a detailed name like …" she paused to think up the most below the salt society she could think up," such as the Winchmore Hill Society or the Totteridge Society – worthy though they may be I am sure,. We are simply the Society and any one in this area who matters knows that."

She looked suspiciously at Keane. "If you are the local bobby, you should know that. Don't you go past our historic Georgian building when you are on your beat … or does another policeman do that?"

Keane tried to inform the women: "As an Inspector, I do not go out on the beat – although I do not underestimate the importance of that. And while the police station where I am based is nearby, our territory is north of here – this street is the boundary line actually – so we do not cover the village or your Society's premises."

"Pity." Was all she said. "As you look to the less-salubrious northern suburbs, I suppose I can forgive your ignorance.

"As well as the Society, I am also on the committee of the local park, which is privately owned and not under the aegis of the LCC, thank goodness. And also chairwoman of the local church PCC. That is of course the C of E church, All Saints. There is a Catholic church here, of course, but we really are not involved with their affairs at all. King Henry Eighth had the right attitude toward Rome."

After this farrago of elitism, snobbery and prejudice Keane felt he had enough and moved on, he hoped, to safer ground, but with one final question.

"You clearly have devoted much of your life to this highly worthy charitable work."

She nodded in an imperial manner.

"Did you come across any other residents of the street in your work? Maybe serving on the same committee as you? "

Priscilla Parry indicated by a frosty look that she did not serve on anyone, she was the one who was served on. "Only one, Mr Ruane is also on the church committee, his knowledge of finance is invaluable in these times where even the Church of England has to tighten its belt as it were."

Keane notice that her earlier slip of calling Mr Ruane 'William' had been quickly papered over. But she could not disguise the fact that the ice in her voice melted slightly when she spoke of Mr Ruane.

He decided to pander to her perceived status: "Well, Mrs Parry, you have certainly helped me to understand the workings of local society –and of the Society."

She nodded gracefully to acknowledge his joke, if that was what it was.

"I think we can now move on."

"What about later on, Mrs Parry. You said neither you nor Mr Parry attended the trial because you stopped any involvement?"

She smiled a rather self-satisfied smile. "When you come from a well-connected family like mine, Inspector, you can quietly and tactfully make sure that you are not involved in any - shall we say - unpleasantness. And having one's husband appear in a sordid murder trial, is most certainly a situation that I did not want to happen."

She looked around almost as if someone unsuitable was listening to her, then continued, "my godfather is …

well, let us say he is at the top of the legal profession. I met with him in his Chambers and asked him to deal with the potential embarrassment that would come from Matthew being in the dock. He is such a sweet man – he just told me to stop worrying and it would be done."

Keane assumes the reference to a 'sweet man' was to her godfather and not her husband. He shook his head, "but Mrs Parry your husband would not have been in the dock! He was called, as I understand it, as a witness to attest to Lizzie Steet's state of mind."

She smiled patronisingly at Keane. "Yes, that is what Matthew said to me as well. You are both so naïve.

"Dock … witness stand … courtroom - whatever it is that you policemen call it. I was not having any member of my family making an appearance there!"

Keane gave up on that thread of questioning. She really was an impossible woman.

"And afterwards?" asked Keane.

"Once again, you did not listen. There was no 'afterwards' as the affair was nothing to us. Other than it meant we had to delay selling our house as the property values slumped due to that stupid boy killing Elizabeth."

Keane thought that Mrs Parry was chancing her luck talking like that with Steet pointing a gun at them all.

But Steet just laughed, "Lizzie had you summed up Mrs P. She always said you were a silly woman. A stupid stuck-up snob.

"Poor Matt, she used to say. Fancy coming home after a worthwhile day saving lives at the hospital to that old bag telling him she married beneath him."

Steet turned to Matthew Parry. "She loved going

round and playing for you, said it cheered you up and you nearly looked happy when she did that.

"And she didn't stop coming round because she saw your ... boyfriend. It was because she didn't realise that everyone else knew, and stayed away because she was scared she would somehow accidentally reveal your secret."

Mrs Parry ignored Steet completely. "Inspector, we had hoped to have moved away from here by now – to Worcestershire where, as I mentioned, my family comes from and where we can fit into proper society. But as I say, the values have not fully recovered. And Matthew keeps putting barriers in the way."

Matthew Parry looked defensive. "My work revolves round London hospitals – there is no transplant unit or facilities in Worcestershire."

She waved her hands in dismissal, "don't be so stupid!"

Keane reflected that the word stupid appeared to be used for anyone who disagreed or questioned her imperious statements.

"There are jobs for surgeons in the Worcester District Hospital that you could do. I am sure they would like an extra hand in ... well, I don't know. Maybe the casualty department. Uncle Hector – he's Lord Bringsty, actually – is Chairman of the Board of Trustees, so he can fix you up."

This was too much for Tristan Thorpe. "You stupid, stupid woman! Do you realise your husband is one of the top heart surgeons in the country, probably in the world. And you want to shunt him off to patch up kids who have grazed their knees in the school playground!

"Nothing wrong with that," she sniffed. "That's what doctors do, isn't it. Anyway, we are moving there when I say so, and that's the end of the matter.

"My father bought the house for me when Matthew was a penniless medical student. So it is my house not his, and my decision not his. We will move back to Worcestershire, to become part of a more ordered and civilised society, when I say and that is the end of the matter."

Parry just sat there miserably and Keane reflected that, even though he was in charge in his operating theatre, in the greater theatre of life, Mrs Parry was correct. She held the purse strings and he would have to go where she said.

Keane had heard enough of Mrs Parry's rather shrill voice and overbearing manner – he turned to Frances Hawkins. "You obviously got on well with Lizzie. What is your story?"

CHAPTER 11
A writer's tale

Frances Hawkin's story

The classroom angel is sighing
She once was the teacher's pet
Now she sits alone in the classroom
Trying her best to forget

The classroom angel is crying
She sits next to his empty desk
The boy of her dreams has left her
Though she gave him her very best

"I didn't ask anything from her, didn't want anything from her. Lizzie used to go to me for advice, as someone who would listen to her. I just gave her some ... stability ... I guess you could call it in the crazy world she inhabited."

Frances Hawkins was unusual amongst the residents of the street in that Keane could see she was clearly a genuinely nice person. That was probably why she did not fit in with the others and was rarely invited to the parties and soirees that took place.

Although they all tended to look down on her, and her relative lack of money, Frances was probably the most talented person in the street. As an author, her work would almost certainly outlive and outlast the sci-fi dramas and puppet shows that the Raymonds pushed out.

She had lived alone in the relatively modest house at the top end of the street for as long as anyone could remember. Indeed, modesty was the word that most people applied to Frances Hawkins. Her house, her lifestyle and her whole demeanour was quiet and low key.

The novels she wrote under her pen name were very successful, but only her agent and lawyer knew her true identity. It was a secret she jealously guarded, and no one in the street, or in the wider world, had an inkling of the truth. Indeed, most of those in the street assumed that she was a small time author, not the literary success story that she actually was. In addition, she had also skilfully adapted three of her novels into a highly acclaimed television series of the sort the BBC excelled in, featuring actors who were not stars, but simply professionals who knew how put on a good performance.

Keane saw in Frances Hawkins the type of person who was often invaluable to police investigations – a witness who saw much and gave a detailed and honest account of what had happened.

"So you saw a lot of Lizzie, Miss Hawkins?"

"Well, long before my writing became successful, I was a teacher at the school where Lizzie was a pupil. So I knew her as a child, and even after she grew up she used to go to me for advice, as someone who would listen to her. She had a difficult time at home with parents who did not understand her ..."

Mrs Ruane broke in, "I certainly did understand her. She was a perfect daughter until she came under the influence of him," pointing accusingly at Jim Steet.

"Please! Mrs Ruane, keep quiet until it is your turn!"

"You seem to be hand-in-glove with him, Inspector. A strange attitude for a policeman, standing up for a convicted murderer who cheated the gallows against the victim's mother's wishes."

"Mrs Ruane, none of us asked to be here, we were all tricked by Jim Steet into coming. But now we are trapped, he has a gun …"

"Two guns and enough bullets for all of you if I am provoked," butted in Steet.

"… OK, two guns, and a wish - a quest - to find out who killed your daughter if you accept Steet's assertion that he did not do it."

Mrs Ruane opened her mouth to argue further, but Keane angrily told her to keep quiet.

"Miss Hawkins, please continue while Mrs Ruane keeps her mouth shut."

She smiled at this. Keane suspected no one usually dared say that to Mrs Ruane.

"As I was saying, she had a difficult time at home, but always a close relationship with Jim. As I tried to say in court and was silenced, they obviously cared for each other – I saw that when they both came round."

"Both?" queried Keane.

"Yes, I used to let them meet at my home so they could have some time together. I would be in my study writing and they would be in the garden room playing music and talking."

"Disgraceful!" said Mr Ruane. "We never knew that! How dare you be party to such behaviour behind our backs!"

Frances Hawkins looked at Keane. "What Mr Ruane does not mention is that they were married then, so I hardly think I can be accused of keeping a disorderly house."

"They were married and had to come to you to be together?" Keane was puzzled.

"Yes, even though they were married, the house they

had planned to buy had fallen through – I believe the modern word is 'gazumped'. So as a temporary measure, Lizzie was still at home and Jim was staying with friends. By then his family had moved away and he had nowhere to stay nearby.

A strange arrangement, Keane thought, with a married couple forced to meet clandestinely at a neighbour's house as they could not live together.

Keane thought for a moment: "So if you taught Lizzie, you also taught Jim as they were at school together?"

"Yes, that's correct Inspector, I knew and taught them both." She looked across at Thorpe. "And Tristan too. She and you were our star pupils - and Lizzie was the teacher's pet, as I remember it."

Tristan smiled ruefully. "Yes, but it was a poisoned chalice for me, as I was expected to do well and work harder that all the others instead of having fun. I would rather have been in the schoolyard with the bad boys like Jim, not in the classroom studying for my big school entrance exam."

Keane turned back to Frances Hawkins. "Jim was a bad boy at school?

"Oh, not bad, just naughty! Whenever there was trouble or a scrap, he would be in the thick of it. He was often absent from class as he was in detention!

"But one thing was good about him was that he looked after Lizzie. Even in those days, she was his special friend. It was quite unusual really as, in the main, the boys stayed together in their little groups, and the girls did the same."

She looked across at Jim and smiled at him. "Inspector, that's why I know that he did not murder her. He wouldn't have … he couldn't have. But someone did - and that someone must be in this room."

Keane nodded. "Thank you Miss Hawkins. We'd better move on now."

"And what about the day Lizzie died?" asked Keane. "Tell me about that ..."

"As has been said already, Tuesday is the script day for one of my novels that is being filmed, so I was at the Television Centre from very early – about eight am – until about seven at night.

"Indeed, it would have been exactly seven when I stopped as most of the crews are highly unionised and at seven they go onto triple pay, so the producers always ask us to stop.

"We were recording a new novel adaptation as the last was a great success and we now have an increased budget! I always like to be around during recording in case some of the script doesn't work out on the day ... then I can rewrite it on the spot.

"Anyhow, I digress. By the time we closed up the set and I took the Tube back from the Centre, it must have been close to nine o'clock. As soon as I crossed the main road and could look down the street, I could see something had happened."

"Was it obvious?" Keane asked.

"Oh, yes! The house was all lit up, there were police cars outside and a lot of ... commotion is the word I would use.

"I went down to see what had happened, but one of the policemen stopped me. Wouldn't tell me anything other than that there had been an incident at the house and I couldn't go any further. He took my name and address and sent me back.

"I went home, and as I could not get near the house, I was so anxious, I telephoned the Ruane's. Bill answered and said 'Lizzie's been murdered by that swine Jim Steet' and hung up."

Keane asked, "are you sure those were his exact words?"

"Yes, Inspector. I could hardly forget them, could I? It was so unexpected and shocking. I went and had a stiff drink and … well … I went to bed. It had been a long and tiring day at the studios and there was nothing I could do.

"The next day, I heard on the radio that they had arrested Jim. I went down to the house but neither of the Ruane's would see me. In fact, I never saw them at all after that until the trial. They seemed to disappear from sight."

"But you did see them at the trial?"

"Yes, Inspector, unlike most of the others, I was at the trial and gave evidence as I thought it was important - and there was no one to stop me." She looked at Matthew Parry who averted his gaze and looked down as the glass of wine – it was his third - Keane noticed.

Keane returned to something Frances Hawkins had said earlier, "you said you were silenced in court. What did you mean by that?"

"Well, Jim's defence man – the idiotic Brantford – seemed to ask questions that the prosecution could have but he saved them the trouble. Often asking things that put Jim in a bad light as he could only answer negatively."

Miss Hawkins paused. "In fact, I will change my mind – I don't think Brantford was an idiot. He was very clever in the way he framed his questions to incriminate Jim so that however he answered, he was damned.

"It seemed like he was the prosecutor not the defence lawyer at times. For example, you asked about when I was silenced. That was typical. Brantford asked me if they ever argued, and my answer was yes, but it was just the way they were and it was never fierce or violent.

"But all I got to say was 'yes' and he stopped me, looked at the jury and said 'as you hear, they argued frequently and violently'. And when I tried to correct the impression, he told me that was all and I could leave the witness stand."

"Didn't the Judge intervene?"

"No, not all. It was no wonder Jim was convicted - the Jury were practically ordered to do so in the Judge's summing up."

"And quite rightly," said Mrs Ruane.

Keane was exasperated at her interruptions. "Will you please shut up Mrs Ruane!"

Jim Steet had listened to Frances Hawkins carefully. At Mrs Ruane's outburst, he raised his gun and made as if to fire it!

"Well done, Inspector, no one ever dares to tell her to shut up - and they should do because she is a bitter, evil old cow."

He looked at the now-silent woman. "I've a good mind to shoot you now just to save time. But I won't. Unlike my trial, this is a fair one and all the facts need to be exposed before a verdict is announced and the sentence carried out."

He smiled at Frances Hawkins. "Thank you Miss H, you were one of the few people who treated us fairly."

"And did things change afterwards?"

She laughed at Keane's question. "Did things change afterwards? No, Inspector Keane, not really.

"The Ruanes simply disappeared from view and we never saw them, but all the other happenings in the street continued. Unlike the others, I was not part of the various drinks parties and bridge evenings. But I still saw them in the street as we went about our daily business.

"Of course, I saw Ray and Jilly at work, though not that often – it is such a huge place. I saw Matthew a fair number of times as, like me, he often walked up to the village for a coffee in the morning.

"And like me, he was alone as Priscilla was away most of the time at her various charity events and functions. Matthew was tied up with his work at the hospital. And Tristan was in New York most of the time, as he told you. So, Inspector, the same but different, if that makes sense."

"Thank you Miss Hawkins. Now Mr Ruane, would you like to have your say ..."

Frances Hawkins spoke up again: "Oh, there was one thing I want to mention."

"Yes, carry on."

"I said I didn't see the Ruanes after the trial. Well, I did see Mrs Ruane once. She was walking along the street and I greeted her, but she was in one of her rages."

"At you?"

"No, at the court, the law, the appeal court ... I forget the whole range of people she was ranting about."

"Why?"

"Oh. Sorry. I did not explain, she had just heard that Jim Steet had been reprieved and his sentence reduced – if that is a reduction – to life. Not that he would have been hanged anyway, given that abolition was in the pipeline and the death sentence was ended for all practical purposes.

"Anyhow, she was furious, and I remember that she said to me he had cheated the hangman and if she could get at him she would hang him herself."

Keane looked at Mrs Ruane who said nothing, perhaps chastened by Keane's outburst at her.

"Maybe she was angry that the man she believes to be her daughter's murderer had escaped the gallows?"

"Yes, I guess so, but I cannot explain … it seemed more than that."

Keane looked at Mr Ruane. "It is your turn now - please continue."

CHAPTER 12
Our little girl ~ Part 1

Mr Ruane's story

You want her to have everything she sees
You think that she should get everything she needs
But she is travelling far too fast to stop
There's just winners never losers cos she's heading for the top

You'd better wave and say goodbye
Wave and say goodbye
Wave and say goodbye to
Your little girl

"She was always my little girl", said Mr Ruane, ignoring the frigid look from his wife. "She could have done better than him," he nodded dismissively at Steet.

"Once we took her away from the local school, we sent her to the best schools in the area, and we made sure she mixed with the best sort of people.

"We certainly hadn't paid all that for her to go off with some ... lad ... from a road on the other side of the hill."

The bitterness in his voice was undisguised and, paradoxically, almost coarse.

"We found the right place for our little girl - she went to Mrs Lyne's school at the top of the hill. They learned dancing and other suitable activities for young ladies, not rough games like at the other place."

He paused and looked at Jim Steet. "Unfortunately, she kept up with some of the children from the local school – including him – and that was something I always will blame myself for."

Mrs Ruane added, "yes, I told him at the time it was a bad idea to allow her to go to a common school, but he didn't listen, always trying to save a few pounds in false economy.

"Of course, we know that millions of ordinary children may well go to those places, but our daughter was not one of millions, or an ordinary child, she was one of a kind."

Mr Ruane picked up the story of her schooling. "Then when she was old enough, she went to St Gertrude's - which is, as you will know, Inspector - one of London's top girls schools.

"Priscilla - Mrs Parry - helped us to gain a place for her - their admissions policy is very selective."

"I was pleased to help, William," she murmured. "I am one of the school's trustees, Inspector."

Keane felt like saying he would have been surprised if she had not been a trustee. The woman seemed to be a professional at the role.

He motioned for Mr Ruane to continue, resisting the urge to call him Bill. "Mr Ruane, We are perhaps getting away from what happened. From how she was in the days and weeks leading up to her death – and the day she died."

"I am sorry to say that she changed," said Mr Ruane. "Once she left St Gertrude's, she said she did not want to go to University, even though Priscilla had arranged a near-certain place for her at LMH – that's Lady Margaret Hall, an all-ladies college in Oxford," he added patronisingly, assuming Keane did not know.

"And you are on the Governing Body?"

Said Keane, wishing to pre-empt a further statement of Pricilla Parry's activities and save time.

Mrs Parry merely nodded graciously.

"Then Ray Raymond over there put the idea of being a model into her head, a disgraceful interference in our family plans."

Ray Raymond shook his head. "I say, Ruane, that is complete rubbish! It was Jilly who first remarked that she had such nice hands and then got her a job modelling for a hand cream company."

Jilly Raymond said, "yes, Ray can't take the credit for her success as a hand artiste. I was the who gave her a start in the career."

"I was not wishing to give credit, Mrs Raymond, but to apportion blame," said Mr Ruane dryly. "The thought of our daughter as a mere model was not something we planned for her. We had her marked down for better things more in keeping with our position in society."

Mr Ruane said to Keane. "As you can see, she went in a totally unsuitable direction, prompted by the Raymonds, and then took up again with Steet over there when we thought we had removed him from her circle of acquaintances.

"We were very annoyed and tried all we could to persuade her to take up the university place offered. Once she was up at Oxford, I know she would have met a more suitable boyfriend."

Keane felt they had heard enough about Lizzie's fall from grace and tried to focus on the immediate prelude to her death.

"And what about the day of the murder, the day she died?" asked Keane. "Tell me about that …"

"We were out of town at a charity event that Priscilla had asked us to attend in her place. We came back late afternoon and ..."

Mrs Ruane stopped him. "Do we have to go through all the details again. It is very distressing for me."

Keane was not about to let them off the hook. They seemed quite happy to go on about how she had been corrupted by the Raymonds and Jim Steet, so he was determined they could also give their account of the day of the murder.

"I need to hear the details from each of you. Please continue Mr Ruane."

"We arrived home about half past five and Mrs Ruane went into the kitchen to make a cup of tea. I went upstairs to change ..."

"You didn't go in here?"

"Well. obviously not, or I would have found the body, not Steet."

"Obviously."

"Then the doorbell rang and it was Steet. Pretended he had not been here earlier and asked if he could see Elizabeth."

"He had to ask if he could see his own wife?" said Keane incredulously.

"Indeed, Inspector. We had very strict rules about where and when they could see each other.

"Then just a few seconds later, he ran into the Kitchen. He stood there for a second, then shouted to us that she was lying in here – dead."

"What did you do?"

"We both went into shock. We just sat there in a daze

and couldn't move. Steet disappeared, and a few moments later we heard his voice and that of the Colonel. After a few more moments, the Colonel came in and, without speaking to us, picked up our phone and called 999.

"I heard him say there had been an accident and ask for an ambulance and then for the police."

Keane turned to the Colonel: "Is that right?"

"Yes. As soon as I saw her I knew she was dead. So I left Jim in here and went to the Kitchen - as I told you earlier, they were both useless, just sitting there like zombies. I called the medics and the police. And went back in here and stayed until they all arrived - seemed like dozens of 'em – ambulance men, policemen as so on."

Keane turned back to Mr Ruane: "You must have gone into the room in the end?"

"Yes, once the shock had worn off. She was lying stretched out on the sofa over there. Actually not that one – they replaced it, after… afterwards," he added when he saw the Chadras shifting uncomfortably on the sofa.

"How was she lying?" asked Keane.

"Good grief, Keane, don't you ever give up! She was lying there in the way you'd expect a girl who had been poisoned by her so-called husband. Stretched out on the sofa, with her hands up by her neck as she obviously had been trying to stop him giving her the poison."

Jim Steet said in a dangerously quiet voice, "you could say that lie in court, but you might not want to repeat it when you are here with me pointing a gun at you."

Keane motioned to him to calm down. "Just wait, Jim. I want to get at the truth as much as you - and threatening anyone more that you are doing will not help."

Keane turned back to Mr Ruane once again: "What puzzles me is the note that you found."

"Ah, yes, the final bit of evidence that he murdered

her. Next to her body no less, a damning document if ever there was one, filled with threats and malice and written by Steet."

"I know you believe he is a bad person. But do you think he is stupid, Mr Ruane?"

"What a stupid question in itself, Inspector! No, he is evil and a murderer. But not stupid – in fact damnably clever in the way he seduced our daughter."

"So, having obtained the poison in a way that no one has ever traced and somehow persuaded your daughter to take it, he then leaves a note beside her body that incriminates him. Seems very stupid to me."

"Ah, well, he made that fatal error in the heat of the moment."

"And having done so, when he came back later to pretend to discover the body, and he was alone for a few seconds at least, he still left it there and did not remove it."

"I assume he was still not thinking straight."

"Hmm. And explain again why you did not call the police when Jim came running in."

"I told you, we were totally shocked. So Steet ran off to the Colonel and, as stated, he was the one who dialled 999 and called the police."

Keane said: "My officers from the local station came first and, as I remember from the short time I was involved with the case, you told them: 'my daughter has been murdered by her husband after they had an argument'. That's right isn't it?"

"The precise words I used, yes."

"What happened then?"

"More and more police came and spent time on all sorts of things … photographs, measuring and such like. Then they took away her body and sealed off the room.

We were not allowed inside. And then they took Steet away and the next morning there was an announcement that he had been charged."

"Did the police tell you that they were going to charge him?"

"Not as I remember. We heard it on the news that morning."

Jim Steet spoke up: "Just to get the facts about the note straight, the strange thing is that I never saw it when I first went in. Or I do not remember seeing it.

"As the Inspector said, had I murdered her …" he halted over the word 'murdered'.

"… I would have removed the note. But as I tried to say at the trial and was stopped, in actual fact I would swear it wasn't there when I went in with the Colonel, I would have noticed it."

He looked accusingly at Mr Ruane.

"That's right, Keane," said the Colonel. "Saw the note later but don't remember it when we first went in. Odd that."

Keane decided to confront Mr Ruane.

"If I had been in court and heard what I have just heard, I would ask you under oath whether you or Mrs Ruane who put the note there. 'Planted it' as the saying goes."

Mr Ruane sputtered, "a damned cheek suggesting that. It was the lad, and that is an end to it. I've a good mind to sue you for slander, Keane."

"Well, as this is a court, albeit a forcibly assembled one, then all that is said is privileged and you can't sue me. Don't be ridiculous."

The Colonel piped up again. "It's now a long time ago and my memory is not what it was, but if it helps, I think it was just folded."

"So?"

"Well if it was a note written by Steet, as she was lying there having been poisoned by him, would she have just folded his angry note? More likely screwed it up!"

Keane reflected that there were so many unusual things about the case all stacking up to what amounted to a conspiracy to convict Jim Steet.

Keane changed tack again. "Tell me about the trial, Mr Ruane."

"The trial was as fair as it could be given he was guilty as hell," started Mr Ruane.

"Wasn't establishing his guilt or not rather the point of the trial? 'asked Keane.

"Not at all. The trial was to show his guilt to all and to shame him into admitting his guilt publicly – something that did not happen – although the lawyers did their best to trap him into a confession."

"But, Mr Ruane, for a start his defence counsel had a duty was to present Jim Steet in the best light he could - even if he was guilty of the murder."

"Inspector Keane, you do not understand, we all wanted to make sure justice was done, not to let Jim Steet off the hook … or keep his neck out of the noose."

Keane sat for a moment nonplussed. He did not know how to question the Ruanes. The couple would have been ideal recruits for the Inquisition, seeing their job as burning heretics - rather than finding out whether a person actually was a heretic.

He tried again, "I have not heard any forensic evidence that actually connected Jim Steet to Lizzie's death?"

Mr Ruane corrected him, "Elizabeth, not Lizzie please.

He was with her, no one else was around and she was poisoned. And the police found a note by her body saying that they were always arguing. And I can tell you - and told the court - she was sometimes frightened by him.

"No doubt about it, he threatened her and then killed her in an argument. That is what I believe you police chappies call an open and shut case, isn't it."

"We prefer to have a motive for Jim to kill her, evidence that he bought the poison, and evidence that he forcibly administered it despite her fighting him off - or that he administered it by subterfuge. None of these appear to be the case."

Mr Ruane looked slightly discomforted by Keane's comment, but Mrs Ruane was unable to keep quiet.

"He killed her because he is crazy, it doesn't matter exactly where the poison came from, he got it. And he must have forced her to take it because no daughter of mine would take poison voluntarily.

"That is the all evidence we and the Judge and Jury needed to find him guilty. He is only here because some obscure psycho-babbler said he is crazy. And a load of liberal do-gooders stopped hanging murderers – which is what they all richly deserve."

"Well, Mrs Ruane, in the eyes of the law, being crazy – if that was what the court-appointed experts judged him to be – is a very good reason to be reprieved. Anyway, you need to remember that in England we do not hang anyone anymore, even crazy people."

"Well, we should!" With that piece of logic, she sat down and glared at Jim Steet as if she was hoping that looks could kill.

"And afterwards?" asked Keane.

"Well, we waited for the day of the execution so that we could celebrate. But as you know, this did not happen, and we are devoting our efforts to having the reprieve overturned ."

"I'm only a policeman, not a jurist, but I think that is a legal impossibility."

"Priscilla has been very helpful introducing us to some of her highly-connected relatives and we have hopes of a private members bill in the house that will allow a specific case to transcend the nonsense of the reprieve."

Keane almost gasped. He looked at Priscilla Parry who turned her head away in a gesture of smug superciliousness.

"I have never heard of such a thing," said Keane weakly. Despite his years of dealing with a whole cast of bad, evil and plain crazy people, he felt out of his depth at the Ruane's hatred of Steet.

"It will happen, we have been assured of that by … well, I cannot repeat a name but someone who has the power do enact it."

Jim Steet spoke up: "Well, it is not going to happen because you are all here in this room, and by the time this night is over, we will find out who killed Lizzie and we won't need a hangman as I will kill them!"

Mr Ruane turned to Keane, "Do you need any more proof that he is a murderer. He has killed once and obviously will kill again. Do something about it, won't you!"

Keane had heard enough of the bumptious and know-all Mr Ruane. He motioned to Mrs Ruane to speak.

CHAPTER 13
Our little girl ~ Part 2

Mrs Ruane's story

The lights come on   The star appears
She's all that they desire
And in a while   Her gleaming smile
Will set their hearts on fire

The camera clicks   The flashgun fires
She was blinded by the light
Stranded in another world
With all those lonely nights

"She was always *my* little girl", said Mrs Ruane, ignoring the look from her husband. "Now that, at last, I am allowed do say a few words."

Jim Steet did not like that. "A few words! We have heard far too much of your interruptions so far, not a few words!

"You spent your life trying to make her fit what you wanted – what you would have like to have been. Then when she wanted to be herself, you fought against it.

"Not the best school for her, but the school that would sound best when you strutted around at your parties telling how Lizzie was at St Gertrude's. The school for snobbery filled with trainee snobs learning how to look supercilious, how to talk down to others and how to find a rich husband."

He paused, and that gave Mrs Ruane the opportunity to re-establish her momentum.

"As you can tell by the common tone of Jim Steet in the corner, I fear that, as Mr Ruane admitted, the decision to send her to a local school, even for a short time, was a terrible mistake.

"That is where she met the man who would murder her. Indeed, there were all sorts of common children there - all of whom were future criminals in all probability, and most certainly were not the sort of children we wanted our daughter to associate with.

"I would remind you, Inspector, that Jim Steet lived in the road on the other side of the hill. Nasty cramped houses, no doubt filled with damp and worse - not like the spacious, detached houses in this street at all."

She said the word 'detached' as if it was somehow an insult, thought Keane. He tried yet again to get her to talk about the day of the murder.

She had one last blast of vitriol: "School for snobs, indeed. If that is so, Mr Jim Steet over there went to a school for murderers!"

"And what about the day of the murder, the day Lizzie – Elizabeth - died?" asked Keane. "Tell me about that ..."

"Like my husband said, we were at a charity event that Mrs Parry arranged for us to go to. It was a favour to her and we met some very influential people. I can't tell you the names, Inspector, I am sure you will understand. Those sorts of people move in circles where it is not done to mention who-is-who, so we were quite at home there."

Keane said in as sarcastic tone as he could manage: "most impressive, Mrs Ruane, I will not ask more." She nodded in an imperious manner that she had borrowed from Mrs Parry.

"So , when you returned at five-thirty ..."

"Oh yes, Mr Ruane went upstairs to change for dinner, as we always do, in fact. We like to keep up certain standards even in these horrid modern times, and I went into the kitchen to see what Amy had left us."

"Amy?" asked Keane.

Jim Steet interrupted Mrs Ruane. "They have a part-time woman – they like to call her their cook or maid depending on who they are trying to impress at the time. In fact, she is a nice widowed lady from my old road who goes there three days a week to cook dinners and also to clean."

"As I was saying before I was interrupted, I went to see what Amy had prepared, and then I heard the doorbell and Mr Ruane letting Jim in.

"As he told you, we were very strict about visiting and he was allowed three evenings a week when he could see her. Although they clearly broke their word with their assignations at Frances Hawkin's house, no doubt for improper activities."

Frances Hawkins was about to speak out, no doubt in protest, but Keane held up his hand and gestured for Mrs Ruane to continue.

"Then, a few moments later ..."

"Do you mean by that a few minutes or a few seconds?"

"I suppose thirty seconds. And then we heard Steet say something and he ran into the Kitchen shouting that Elizabeth was dead … as if he did not already know that as he had killed her.

"And then, as my husband said, Steet ran off to fetch the Colonel. And it was the Colonel who called the police. We were just too upset to do anything and sat in the kitchen in shock. As for Steet, he was obviously in a trembling panic from the murder to do anything."

"And then?"

"There is not really much more to tell. When we had

recovered, we came in here …"

She dabbed at her eyes - for effect not genuine emotion - Keane suspected.

"… and within a few minutes the ambulance men and then police came and they more or less ordered us to leave the room …"

There was another eye-dabbing pause.

"We went back into the Kitchen and a policewoman made me a cup of tea, and Mr Ruane had a small tot of whiskey. All the while we could hear the police fussing around, Then they called us into the study on the other side of the hall one at a time to ask a lot of questions. What a cheek, treated like suspects in our own house!

"We explained that they had been arguing and pointed out the note we had seen and read that was by the body. The police detective seemed more annoyed that we had touched it than interested in its contents.

"But I told him quite sharply that if he had found his daughter murdered by her husband, and a note next to her, he would have done the same.

"But being just a policeman and not a gentleman, he did not have the grace to apologise. Such an ignorant man.

"Anyway, in the end they were finished, and we were left in the house to mourn.

"The next day we heard they had raided Jim Steet's house and arrested him before he could escape. And that was it."

Jim shook his head. "They didn't raid my house and I wasn't about to escape anywhere as I had no idea that they were going to arrest me. They came round and questioned me - it was Inspector Lattice and two other detectives.

"They made a big thing of the argument we were

meant to have had, and the note which they claimed I had written threatening her. They didn't show it to me or say what it was in it.

"In fact I never saw the note at any time. When I was in prison awaiting trial I asked Brantford if I could see it or a copy of it. He said it was so painful to the Ruanes that he had admitted its contents and authorship by me to the prosecution. And that they had therefore agreed not to submit it in open court."

"Have you ever seen the note – maybe later? Asked Keane.

No, Inspector. I believe it was eventually returned to the Ruanes - along with other personal items – and including her wedding ring," said Jim.

"Well you don't think they would give her wedding ring to her murderer!" Mrs Ruane said sarcastically.

"And where is the letter now? Asked Keane although he could guess the answer.

Mr Ruane looked at him in astonishment: "We destroyed it. What else would we do with it. And we threw the wedding ring in the rubbish bin as you might expect."

Keane looked at Jim, concerned that the Ruanes taunting might drive him over the edge.

Matthew Parry intervened, "Ignore them Jim, they are trying to upset you." He looked across the table at Mr and Mrs Ruane. "You are simply shameful, both of you."

Priscilla Parry turned on him. "Don't you dare say that to Lizzie's parents. With all they put up with from Jim Steet, they were quite right in destroying everything that reminded them of him - and of his bad influence on that poor girl."

There was along silence broken by Jim. "Come on Inspector – ask them about the trial."

❧⌾❧

"So, let me tell you about the trial ..." Mrs Ruane started to say.

Keane interrupted her. "No, let me ask you about the trial.

"How long had you known Henry Brantford, Jim Steet's defence counsel?"

"What relevance is that to you. How impertinent of you to ask."

Mr Ruane said, in what Keane thought was a rather sulky tone, "my wife has known Henry since she was a child."

Mrs Ruane continued, "Jim had no money so the Government - or whoever it is that pays up in such cases – appointed Henry Brantford to defend him. It was nothing do with us, just a coincidence.

Keane commented: "It was an unfortunate coincidence that should have been stopped by Brantford stepping down."

He had an increasing suspicion that Brantford's appointment had been improperly arranged – but he knew if he challenged Mrs Ruane she would deny it.

While she was speaking, he kept a careful eye on Priscilla Parry as he was sure that she was the 'arranger'. As Mrs Ruane spoke up, a momentary expression of annoyance flickered across Priscilla Parry's face. Not long enough to be apparent - except to Keane.

He decided to return the mater of the mysterious note found by the body.

"I am intrigued by the note that seemingly threatened Lizzie and was surely a prime piece of evidence for the prosecution.

"That has already been explained to you. It was obvious that it was written by Jim and Brantford wanted to save us the pain of hearing our daughter being threatened by her eventual murderer."

Was it signed by Jim? And what about the date? When was it written? I am wondering if in truth was a actually a very old letter that you or Mr Ruane left by the body."

Mrs Ruane turned on Keane angrily. "That is just twisted logic that some defence lawyers would use to try to get him off the hook."

Keane decided reluctantly that it was time to move on, he had found out more than the Ruanes wanted to be found out, and time was passing.

Jim Steet interjected: "Just one last thing on the note. Even you, Inspector Keane, are missing the real point: I would never have written a threatening letter to Lizzie. Signed or unsigned - and not at any date in the calendar. That is why I know it was a fake."

Fake or not, it was certainly a puzzle – and one that would have helped to solve the murder, thought Keane.

"So, Mrs Ruane, afterwards, when the trial was all over and Jim Steet was found guilty?"

"Oh, then we were very much looking forward to the day when we would know that our daughter had been avenged.

"But he cheated the gallows by feigning insanity, so now we are to having to get the reprieve overturned."

Keane looked at her incredulously. As he had thought earlier, he had met quite a few crazy people in his time. Some perpetrators and others victims, but he had not met many like Mrs Ruane and her crazy notions of crime and punishment.

Reversing a reprieve was surely totally impossible any-way… but more than that. Steet's conviction had been at the very end of the death penalty in the UK, so he would not have hanged at the time. It had now been abolished, and there was no way even the most heinous mass murderer would be executed.

Now Mrs Ruane had finished speaking, she turned away, closing her eyes as if dismissing the present reality.

"I really am very tired of all this. Just get us released, that's what you're paid for isn't it. Do your job."

In a way, thought Keane, she was right, that was his job, to get them all out of the room alive and unharmed.

He turned to Steet. "You've heard all that has been said about what happened. Now I'd like to hear your story - it's your turn to speak."

Jim Steet looked round at them all and said, "not me Inspector. It is time for the twelfth member of the jury.

"Here in spirit and with her apologies for the delay in presenting her evidence."

He gave Mrs Ruane a scathing look. She simply turned her head away.

CHAPTER 14
A voice from the grave

Lizzie's story

The green of summer's a memory
And the grass is windswept white
And that big cold wind is the enemy
That turns the day to night

Outside beyond the distant trees
The shadows shift and turn
But he'll never come to claim her love
No he never will return

Jim Steet took a notebook from his pocket. It was well-worn, leather-covered and dog-eared. But he looked at it lovingly. "It's Lizzies' private diary. The Ruane's found it and hid it from me. I never knew it existed.

"Then, when Miss Hawkins came to see me in prison she told me about it. She was the only of the residents of the street who bothered to visit me.

"By then the reprieve had come through and I was not on 24-hour watch. Instead, I was in the prison hospital. Like a lot of reprieves, I had a kind of nervous breakdown when I knew I would not be hanged after all. Just ten or more years in prison.

"Miss Hawkins came to the hospital visitors facility with warders still watching us there closely all the time. But she managed to tell me that Lizzie once told her she kept a diary and only I would know the place where she kept it hidden."

Suddenly, and unexpectedly, Mrs Ruane leapt up and threw herself at Miss Hawkins, shouting, "you stupid old woman! You do not realise what you have done. Interfering with justice."

Matthew Parry dragged her away with the help of the Colonel who showed a surprising turn of energy.

They pushed her back down on her chair and she sat there muttering as Steet continued.

Keane watched all this and began to pull some of the tangled threads together. It was clear to him that Mrs Ruane had found the diary after her daughter had died - and she hid it as it did not fit her certainty that Lizzie had been killed by Steet.

"Mrs, Ruane, by hiding her diary it was you who were interfering with justice. Why did you hide it? Why didn't you show the police the notebook?"

Mrs Ruane looked at Keane contemptuously, "we wanted to keep her private thoughts out of the gossip columns.," she said in an offhand way. "It had nothing to do with the case."

Keane held up his hand to Steet who had raised the gun, his hand trembling a little with rage.

"Mrs Ruane, it was more than gossip, someone nearly went to the gallows for this. Please continue, Jim."

Jim Steet continued. "Once Miss Hawkins had told me about the diary, I realised what Lizzie meant by something she had said to me … one of the last times ever I saw her." He swallowed and seemed about to lose control, but gritted his teeth and continued.

"She said, 'whatever happens, don't ever forget the place where we hid our notes to each other when we were children.'

"So I decided that I would do whatever I could to get out of prison and find the diary even if it took me years."

He laughed humourlessly, "Which it did. Those long years in prison for something I did not do and made worse by the fact that the real murderer - or murderers - were outside and enjoying life.

"The opportunity came when Sid and Tubby made me an offer when we got a few quiet words in the exercise yard.

"They said they had contacts who would get them out of the prison but they needed someone who knew London and its quieter corners to help them hide up until they got out of the country. If I agreed to that, then I was in with them."

"Why was it not reported that the three of you had escaped?" questioned Keane.

"Well, Inspector, I think it was something to do with the fact that Sid Silverman was not his real name – as I discovered once we got out.

"They were in the secure unit as well, Tubby because, although he was a forger by profession, he had killed his partner in a row over money.

"But Sid was in a different league - had got life for a major espionage plot – I never was told the full story - and wanted to get back to his home country. I never found out where that was.

"So I reckon the powers-that-be do not want the fact that a convicted spy has escaped known to the public - or more likely to his masters.

"So we holed up a flat that I had got lined up – won't tell you how I did that. While we were there, Sid made his plans to skip the country, while Tubby had other plans abroad that I never found out. And I made mine to get Lizzie's diary and to invite you all to this little gathering.

"It couldn't have been easier as Tubby was an expert forger and a real artist at making up new documents. The invites that lured you here looked really good, didn't they!

"It was Sid that told me that this house had been sold

and was a Government safe house. It was not something I knew much about beforehand.

"Anyway, he knew somehow that the house was empty and he and Tubby helped me break in. I found the diary – it was exactly where I knew it would be – while Sid went upstairs for a quite long time, he seemed to be looking for something he knew was also here and was of interest to him. Something to do with the new owners."

Keane wondered what Sid had been up to. Something to follow up when - if - they all got out alive from this siege.

Steet continued: "Once I got back to the flat and read through the diary, I decided exactly what I would do - hold a new trial to find the truth and the real murderer.

"As I said, the details were Sid's idea and he helped me with the plan. He is out of the country now, so they will not catch him. And who knows where Tubby is."

Keane interrupted: "Did you get the Beretta from Sid? It doesn't look like the kind of gun you'd find in a regular 'hunting, fishing, shooting' shop? More professional killer's weapon!"

"Yes, Sid gave it to me – and showed me how to use it." He aimed it at Mrs Ruane. "I won't hesitate to use it if I must."

He held the open diary up to Mrs Ruane. "Anyhow, let's get back to this re-trial. Not very flattering about the two of you, is it.

"But it showed what she thought about me – a very different impression from the one you manufactured for the police and the trial."

"You deserved to hang," she smirked. "You took her away from us. That was like killing her. You deserved to hang for that."

"Mrs Ruane," interrupted Keane in exasperation. "To

marry your daughter against your wishes is not a capital offence - whatever you might wish."

He looked directly at her. "Hiding evidence that would have cleared someone is a terrible thing to do."

She shrugged her shoulders dismissively. "I told you he deserved to die and it was only the stupid appeals Judge, who did not do as he was told, who allowed him ..." she nodded at Steet, "... that allowed him to slip the noose and live."

Keane decided to move on. "That's enough history, now let's get to the diary and Lizzie's evidence."

"Do you want to read it, inspector?"

"No, I think it should be you."

Steet nodded in agreement. He moved further back against the door in the corner of the room so that he could read easily, but still be well away from any attempt to overpower him while he held it.

He opened the diary and started to read quietly and carefully, but the gun was still at the ready.

"I'll read you just a bit to show how Lizzie really felt. It was written in the days when we were going out together, a year before we were married, I remember the time, she went with them down to the South Coast and hated every minute."

What a life. Stuck with my boring parents at the seaside. Nothing to do. Missing Jim a lot. Sitting in the Pier End theatre watching crap performers sing out of tune. Oh, how I wish I was back home in London.

Mrs Ruane yelled, "she didn't write that, you've made it up. She loved being with us at the seaside."

Steet ignored her and continued to read:

Oh what a boring time, stuck with my cow of a mother and having to walk round stupid shops looking at clothes that are only fit for old ladies.

Mind you, they suit her well.

I wish Jim were here to make me laugh or Tristan to be his usual caring self. But no, they are both in London while I roast here on the horrible, pebbly beach.

One day I will be rid of them and be with my darling Jim all the time.

I wish I could escape with Jim to somewhere they cannot bother us any more, to a place where we will get some peace and quiet.

He was only one who ever treated me like a real person as well as ...

He stopped reading suddenly and closed the diary.

"That enough. Really sounds like someone who loved her parents, didn't it," he said sarcastically, looking round the room at all of them.

"End of diary reading for today, there's lots more but I can't read it now. I will give it to you when we are done, Inspector."

"… Does it go up to the day of the murder - the day she died?" asked Keane.

"Not quite, it ends there very suddenly at the end of a page. I can't be sure, but I think there are pages missing," said Steet.

"But it does say a lot about how she felt just a few days before …"

Then, suddenly, unexpectedly, Tristan Thorpe stood up.

Jim Steet turned the gun towards him, threateningly. "Sit down, Tristan."

But he ignored the threat.

"Yes, there were other pages. Three in fact. And I tore them out a few weeks after her death. There was a ghastly party – a wake – held by the Ruanes and I sneaked into the cellar where she hid the diary.

"Don't forget, Jim, that we grew up together, and I knew the hiding place as well as you did. Just that you were in prison and couldn't get to it. But I could."

Jim Steet looked puzzled, the gun wavering a little in his previously-steady hand.

"But why? Why did you want the diary? What was in it that was so important to you?"

After that it all happened so quickly. And Keane realised before Jim Steet did what Tristan Thorpe was getting at. Long before any of the others in the room.

Tristan looked at Jim with an air of scorn, "you always were far sharper than me and with your charm, you always got out of scrapes. Often ones that you had got us into then left me to get the blame or pick up the pieces.

"And the same with girls as we grew up, always charming the prettiest ones while all the time having poor Lizzie to go back to when you were ready."

The gun wasn't wavering anymore and the safety catch clicked off. As Jim began to understand.

"Even after you were married, you still had to cheat on Lizzie, didn't you? She never knew it and it would have broken her heart. But I knew it and determined to make sure she would never know. I wanted her to die happy."

Jim raised the gun.

"All the time I was the one who really cared about her - but she never realised how much. And all the time you were off at clubs and worse when she was at photoshoots and couldn't see what you were up to. You cheated on her time and time again.

"Yes, you kept it well hidden, but I knew."

Keane tensed himself hoping his injured leg would not slow him down too much when the moment came – as it would soon.

"So I went round to see her once when you were away on one of your jaunts, and we spent the night together.

"A night that should have been a lifetime together. But after it, she told me go keep away, to never see her again. I couldn't do that."

Tristan was now close to Jim and Keane guessed what he planned.

"If I couldn't be with her, then no one could. Not you. Not anyone. So I went round that Tuesday saying I wanted to say goodbye forever. She didn't realise that was exactly what I meant.

"I took with me some poison I had got hold of during one of my South American trips looking for antiques for the shop. Had the police bothered to investigate properly, they would have known it was not a poison that you could possibly have got bought here - or anywhere in Europe for that matter.

"But they were blinded by their need for a quick arrest and conviction - and by her parent's tampering with the evidence to frame you.

"I didn't really kill Lizzie, I released her from a life with you and not with me."

Jim's finger closed on the trigger.

"Don't be upset Jim, she never felt a thing. I would not have wanted her to suffer. I loved her too much. We had a toast to old friends. Drink up I said! She did, and was dead in an instant.

"I said goodbye and left her as she was. It was so easy.

"And I never tried to frame you – that was Mrs Ruane's doing. She thought you had done it and wanted to make sure you were hanged.

"Now I will do the job that the hangman was cheated of."

There was a terrible moment of stillness, then Tristan lunged at Jim to get the gun, Jim tried to fire it but Tristan had the strength of a madman – which is what he had become.

As they struggled, Keane hobbled forwards them and tried to grab the gun. The old Colonel also tried, but the two lifelong rivals were locked in a deadly embrace.

There was a shot and Jim slumped down. Quite dead.

Keane grabbed Thorpe and with the Colonel's help, pinioned him while Matthew used his belt to tie Thorpe up.

He didn't struggle. He lay there on the floor totally still, like a man who was as dead as Jim Steet.

There was a shocked silence, broken by Keane.

"The trial's over, everyone. Jim Steet is dead."

He gestured at the body and picked up the Beretta - and also the smaller hand gun - the type often called a 'gamblers gun'. He placed then safely on the table by the door.

Mr Ruane said, in a self-important tone, "you shouldn't have touched those, Inspector! Fingerprints and evidence for the inquest."

Keane turned to Mr Ruane and was about to tell him to shut up when a shot shattered the lock of the door behind him.

Wilshire burst into the room, almost falling as he encountered Steet's body lying just inside the door.

Keane raised his hands to show everything was under control.

"It's OK, Wilshire. Steet is dead and we have his killer safely restrained."

Wilshire looked carefully round the room to examine each person in turn.

"And everyone else is safe and unharmed?"

Keane nodded, "as you can see, all the rest of us are OK."

Wilshire came over to him and whispered a few words in Keane's ear. He looked surprised and motioned for Wilshire to go to the head of the table.

Wilshire looked around the room.

"Please sit down all of you. And listen to me very carefully.

"Before I unblock the front door and let the police and other personnel in to clear up, I need to tell you that the events of this night are now to be forgotten.

"You must understand. This is where it all ends. No inquest. No statements to the police. Just get back to your normal lives. The events of this night are to be forgotten - permanently.

"The case is closed."

Once the police came in, under Wilshire's direction, the now-discharged involuntary Jurors were escorted back to their back to their homes with hostage support officers in tow to deal with any immediate traumas.

Each of them were interviewed in turn as soon as possible – to make sure that the message about not revealing or discussing what took place was firmly reinforced.

Tristan Thorpe was not taken home but to Keane's station to be formally charged with manslaughter.

He was later found guilty. But after intervention by Q5

officials in the closed court, it was decided he would not be charged with murder, and that the case of Lizzie Steet's death would remain on file as murder by Jim Steet.

Jim had no family to argue on his behalf that the decision was a rather unfair and wrong conclusion on his behalf.

And that was very nearly the end of the affair.

Edited Summary of final section of C5 Unit Detective Sergeant Wilshire's report on the night of the siege as filed in C5 archives later.

It was pitch black outside the incident cabin and I could only see the dark outline of the house across the road. Not even a glimmer of light showed from any of the windows Steet had been very thorough in his preparation.

I looked at my watch and decided to give them another ten minutes, then into the house through the basement - the way I guessed Steet had used. Just before the ten minutes were up, and when I had already made my way through the garden of the house, I heard a shot.

It only took a few seconds to reach the door at the back that led from the garden into what would have been the servant's hallway. This door was not secured efficiently and it only took a more few seconds to get through it.

Immediately on my left in the hall was the door leading from there into the Dining Room. This had been well secured, so I shot off the lock and went into the room, almost falling over a body it was Steet's - as I did so.

Chapter 14 - A voice from the grave

The room was quiet, with the various occupants standing still like they were in a waxworks. Keane was standing near to Steet's body, while next to him were two men who I later discovered were Mr Parry and Colonel Templemead-Newson. They were restraining Thorpe who was lying on the floor.

I spoke to Keane and he reassured me that all was now under control. So I unblocked the front door and let the Met police officers, hostage support team, medics and C5 personnel come in. I escorted them into the Dining Room so they could look after the freed hostages, remove the body of Steet and take away Thorpe to custody.

I issued a warning to all in the room and told them that there would be no inquest. No statements. The events of this night were to be forgotten, permanently. The case was closed.

As Keane and I knew, the C5 team would deal with everything. There was no mention of the siege in the press or anywhere of the events of that night under the usual 'D' notice procedures. In addition, all paperwork with local and Scotland Yard police was cleansed by our wash-up team in line with standard procedures.

The classified nature of the case is complicated by the issue of Mrs Parry and her high level contacts and relatives. But this case is far above any influence they might have and has the highest security classification due to ex-C5 operative Keane being involved and even more due to the presence of the POII named 'Trinity'.

That is the end of my report.

CHAPTER 15
The end of the affair

When it is all over
What can you do
Cry for a while
Sigh for a while
But it's the end of the affair
And she is done with you

A few days later Matthew Parry and Templemead-Newson were standing in the Colonel's study overlooking the terrace and enjoying a well-deserved sundowner.

"What I can't understand," said Matthew puzzled, "is all the secrecy about the siege and Thorpe killing poor Jim Steet."

"Aha, I think I know – or can guess – why that is." The Colonel gestured to the terrace.

"Come out to the terrace and enjoy the fresh air and the view. Can't be overheard by that rogue Paton there."

They walked out and looked across the new houses in the near distance and over to the golf course in the far distance.

"As these old houses are sold off one by one, there are ten or twenty little boxes erected in their place. When Lady Newson and I moved here it was all greenery with formal gardens right up to the golf course. Now seems like every time I look another spot of green is gone and there are more houses."

He walked to the edge of the terrace, wanting to be as far away from the house as he could get.

"Anyway, I can tell you a bit more than is general knowledge. Had a chat on the QT with one of my junior officers from the old days.

"Of course, he's now near retirement and in his 50s but is something high up in Military Intelligence."

Matthew Parry looked astonished. "What did he say?"

"Wouldn't go into specifics – wouldn't expect him to either – just said that one of us in the room was a pretty important person to the Government and they would have moved heaven and earth to make sure he was kept safe and secure. That's why all the hush-hush afterwards and us having to swear on scout's honour not to discuss it."

"Good lord. I wonder who it was?"

"Don't know and literally don't have a clue. But only mentioned it to you as I have heard Priscilla making a couple of unfortunate remarks about the affair.

"You are going to have to tell her to shut up or …", he left the words unsaid.

"You know what she's like Colonel, a law unto herself. She won't do as I say, ever."

"Hmm," the Colonel thought for a moment. "Well, I am going to pop in to see that Inspector chap. He seemed pretty clued up. He will sort her out."

The next morning Keane had an unexpected visitor.

"Come in Colonel. Have a seat. What can I do for you?"

"Will come straight to the point, Keane. No shilly-shallying."

Keane groaned inwardly, expecting another of the Colonel's digressions. But no.

"You need to shut Pricilla Parry up before she lets the cat out of the bag. Don't know what the cat is, or the bag for that matter, and don't want to know. Not my business. But the warning we were all given hasn't made any impression with her."

He stood up. "I'm a man of few words, as you know." Keane smiled slightly.

"But I know when things need to be kept under wraps - and that woman needs a good talking to. Needed it for some time in my view!"

The Colonel said goodbye to Keane and, as he walked down the steps to the front of the police station, wondered if Keane was in some way connected to the embargo – if he was the one who was being protected.

But he doubted it. Nice enough chap for a policeman, and had been good at keeping the siege night under control. But not intelligence material. No, not at all. The Colonel could always weigh up a man and tell if he was in that line of business.

So who was the important person? He had a strong suspicion it was Ray Raymond. No one could really be as foolish and empty-headed as that man pretended to be.

In the afternoon Keane paid a call on Priscilla Parry. He knew she would be in as the Colonel's concerns had not been a surprise to him. Keane too had heard rumours of her indiscretion and tipped off Wilshire.

Since then, Q5 operatives had been keeping a quiet eye on the house and its visitors – and checking all telephone conversations.

When Keane had called Wilshire to tell of the Colonel's visit, Wilshire paused to think for an instant, then said, "rather than send one of my enforcers round – yet – would you be willing to have an informal word with her? Give her a last chance."

Keane had agreed.

He pressed the very elegant doorbell push and waited. She came to the door.

"Oh, Inspector ..." she paused as if she could not remember his name, though he suspected she could. "So nice to see you, if unexpected, but I was just going out to a rather important meeting."

Keane knew that was not true. His final update before he arrived - from the surveillance team - was that her afternoon meeting had been cancelled an hour ago due to illness.

"I doubt that Mrs Parry, as I know your meeting has been cancelled."

She looked astounded - and angry. "How did you know that? I have only just found out."

Keane decided subtlety was not going to work on her – a frontal approach and threat that she would understand was needed.

"Because we have you under surveillance and are listening to all your telephone conversations."

"That is illegal!" Her face creased in anger.

"No, not when we have a High Court order signed by the Home Secretary."

He decided to add an innovation of his own. "And we are screening all your post."

She stood there outraged and looked like she was about to slam the door in his face.

"I will be calling some very influential people about this!"

Keane pushed carefully but firmly past her.

"No you won't. As I told you, we listen to and control all your calls. Now, I need to have some very strong words with you."

He walked into the dining room uninvited and sat

down at the head of the table – she followed him, muttering angrily.

"Sit down Mrs Parry and let me give you a warning – no, an order. You were all told you all at the end of the siege by the intelligence Officer that it was not to be discussed at all, and that you were all to forget about it."

He drummed his fingers on the table wanting to give the impression of someone trying to be fair but impatient.

"Look, Mrs Parry, I am going to give you one more chance before things get official and – shall we say embarrassing - for you."

He decided that there was one threat that would mean far more than any from Q5.

"You pride yourself on your connections and knowing the right people. Well, I have tell you that even knowing every single member of the House of Lords will not help you if you persist in disobeying instructions from the intelligence officers on this case. And this goes all the way up to the Home Secretary. Do I make myself clear?"

"So, are you one of the intelligence officers?"

"No, just the local CID officer who has been requested to give you a last unofficial warning before ..." He stopped and left the exact threat unsaid.

She was quiet for a moment.

"Can I know why it is all so important?"

"No. And I don't know either. I suggest you lose all interest in this matter, otherwise you will find your official committees decide they need to replace you with a fresh Chairperson, your invitations to Livery Company dinners dry up, you don't get to attend Royal Ascot ... and so on. I think you can understand what I am saying."

She got up, walked to the door, and pointedly opened it.

"Very well, Inspector Keane, I must do as you say. Please leave now, I find your presence unpleasant."

As he left, she said, "I assume you will call off your spies now?

"They are not spies, and they do not work for me, but I will report our conversation to the relevant officers and they will do what they decide is appropriate."

Keane reported back to Wilshire that he was sure she would now behave.

However, Keane suspected the surveillance would continue for some time afterwards - just to be sure.

A short time after that, Wilshire came round to see Keane to get him to sign the statement about the siege he had given. It was not one that would see the light of day in any regular police files, but it would stay in the relevant Q5 file.

"So, it was not Steet who killed her, despite all that the girl's parents tried to do to prove it was him."

"Lingchi." Said Keane enigmatically.

Wilshire looked puzzled. "Sorry, Sir, I didn't quite catch that."

Keane smiled, but not a humorous smile. "I said Lingchi. In ancient China, Lingchi was death by a thousand cuts. Do you follow me?"

Wilshire nodded, beginning to understand.

"In one sense Tristan Thorpe killed her. But in another sense, Mrs Chadra was actually quite correct - they all did.

"As Mrs Chadra said, the lying, cheating and worse - sickened Lizzie to death and drove her to the brief affair with Tristan - and then drove him to him to murder her."

Wilshire nodded in agreement. He had not always followed Keane's more obscure reasoning of motives for crimes, but this time he could.

"There were, as always, a number of red herrings as things unfolded," said Keane. "I had assumed that the Ruanes sending Mr and Mrs Chadra to Glyndebourne was a ploy to get them out of the way."

Wilshire shook his head. "No, we questioned them closely about that. After a bit of blustering, they admitted it was simply that they wanted to show off the fact that they knew a senior Indian diplomat to their equally snobbish set of acquaintances they met at the opera."

"Makes sense, now I know what they are like.

"But I guess Tristan Thorpe's cock and bull story – more a bull elephant story - about the valuable hunting horn was made up to cover up the fact he never went to auction that day?"

"Oh, he went to an auction as he described it alright – but not on that day! We checked the story and he really did buy the olyphant and made a tidy sum on the deal. But not on the Tuesday in question."

Wilshire paused as if about to impart a secret, but his Q5 training took over.

"I was about to tell you the place where the auction was, but even after all this time, I think that had better stay hidden.

"All I can say is that it is perhaps comforting to know that even the highest and grandest old families have their cashflow problems just like common people."

Keane nodded in agreement. "I have not forgotten the unofficial Q5 motto: Non quaeris, non dico."

He poured them a modest measure of whisky taken from the discreetly locked cupboard behind his desk. He knew it was Wilshire's favourite blend - he had not yet managed to educate Wilshire into appreciating single malts.

"Thanks for your help at the end of the siege. Your dramatic entrance was impressive."

Wilshire sipped appreciatively. "That's OK, Sir. Nice to work with you again, even though you were on the wrong side of the fence as it were this time."

Wilshire looked at Keane and asked a question he had wanted to ask for some time. "Is there any chance you might come back to us, Sir? Now that Harries has gone and all the falsehoods he put out have been refuted."

Keane smiled.

"Well, Wilshire, you know how it is. Maybe I am already back and you don't know it. Because you wouldn't necessarily know, would you!"

They chatted for a few moments about old colleagues and cases then, having finished their whisky, Keane signed the statement.

He held out his hand to Wilshire.

"Good luck, maybe we will meet again on a case, who can tell what the future holds."

Wilshire shook Keane's hand and went down the stairs of Keane's apartment, letting himself out.

Keane looked out through his front room window as Wilshire walked away without looking back. As he had said, you never can tell.

Some time later, Keane met Jean Bridges in the street as he was on his way to interview a witness to an unusually - for his patch anyway - violent robbery.

He had seen Jean from time to time as she still lived in the same house where the events with McKenzie had started. And she was still married to rather boring, rather pompous John.

On previous occasions he had just nodded to her, slightly embarrassed at his memories of the McKenzie case. But this time she crossed the street and walked up to him.

"Good morning, Inspector K, how are you? I see you from time to time, but you always seem to be on the other side of the street, so I thought I would come over to your side."

She looked at him with the direct, inquisitive look he remembered so well.

"Could it be that you are avoiding me? Maybe embarrassed at what nearly happened between us when we all thought John was dead?"

Keane was reminded of her disorienting habit of going straight for the truth. He nodded.

She smiled sympathetically.

"I know how you … we ... felt. But when John reappeared alive, that was the end of it. Wasn't it?"

Keane nodded again, not feeling that he could add anything.

"I suppose there is such a thing as doing too good a job!" She touched his sleeve. "I will never forget what happened and what you did."

She looked at him more closely: "That strange affair in the Avenue a bit ago ... when it was closed off and no one knows to this day why or what happened. Were you involved?"

He laughed, "you know better - and know me even better - than to expect an answer to that question."

She smiled and turned to go - then she stopped and looked back at Keane.

"You should write your memoirs, you know, they

would be fascinating and sell well!"

"Yes, for all the wrong reasons, I think. I can see it now in screaming headlines: 'Secret Life of Intelligence Agent Revealed!'.

"Sounds good!"

"Well, Jean, it can never happen. They would never give permission, and if I did it anyway, there would be a visit from two polite gentlemen in dark suits and that would be the end of it."

"Really?"

"Yes, really. They do not like their secrets revealed." Jean thought for a moment.

"How about the other cases you have been involved in, the less ... special ... ones. They would make a good book as well. I bet that there are plenty of interesting sad, happy or simply weird cases just here in your apparently quiet suburban police station."

"You can say that again," laughed Keane.

"You could talk about those. No one would stop you. I could write about them – I would interview you instead of you doing the interviewing. The memoirs of a suburban policeman instead of a secret policeman!"

Keane smiled at her, "you are always full of ideas, Jean. That is one to consider, maybe."

She walked away leaving Keane, as ever, to watch her departing figure with regret.

A long time later, a messenger rang Keane's doorbell. He handed Keane a large manila envelope. Inside it was an extract from the follow up report on what had happened in the street since the siege. It was unsigned, in the routine manner of all Q5 documents, but Keane recognised Wilshire's style.

Tristan Thorpe was found guilty of manslaughter and will serve 10 years or more years before he can be released. As background, after his parent's death he had taken the family business to new heights and had been one of the most renowned experts of pre-war British art and a visiting Professor of Fine Art at the Royal College. All that was gone now and the business closed as Tristan had been the sole driving force.

The Colonel died in the spring after a short illness. He was 87 and had been in fine form until the end. His military career was more distinguished than he made out, and he had been one of the heroes at Gallipoli during the Great War.

Ray Raymond was enjoying immense success as his sci-fi series had been sold to the USA and was being remade with a huge budget.

Jilly was less fortunate as changing tastes meant that her puppet series had come to an end and Sand Boy was consigned to the backwaters of television history. His fate was to be shown in brief clips in Christmas children's compilations such as 'The Golden Days of Children's TV'. She spent her new free time annoying Ray by trying to help him with his production – a help that was as unwanted as it was unappreciated.

The Chadras had gone back to India and disappeared off the radar completely - which was a great relief to Q5 and the UK Government. Despite Mr Chadra's quiet demeanour, he was not a minor diplomat on a routine posting to the UK. He was 'Trinity', the second in command of India's Intelligence service, and had been sent the UK to nnnnnnnnnnnnnnnnnnnnnnnnnnnnnnn (Ed: redacted under 'D' notice 124/Q5/XR45867). The objective and details of his mission were beyond even the clearance of anyone at Q5 to know. But what they did know – and had very clear orders to implement – was that that fact the Mr Chadra was being held in a siege in London was not something the UK Government wanted known. And he was not to come to any harm - whatever the cost to the other hostages.

Matthew Parry had moved to Worcestershire with Priscilla Parry as she wished. His heart transplant unit – which was totally reliant on his skill – had been shut down. He had taken early retirement and taken up golf. Mrs Parry was making a nuisance of herself as a reactionary appointee to a number of education, hospital and charity boards in the UK and beyond.

Frances Hawkins had written a new novel that further enhanced her pen name's reputation - and it was rumoured it was going to be made into a Hollywood movie with a number of top box office stars in it.

Mr Ruane had been promoted in the bank and was now rarely seen as he was in charge of the bank's expansion into the USA and spent much of his time there. He saw quite a lot of Priscilla Parry who had been appointed a trustee of the Anglo-USA Cultural Exchange Board by her nephew who was British Ambassador there.

Mrs Ruane was a sad case, and spent most of her time in their new house – the one they had bought after selling the old house to the Colonial Office - writing letters to all and sundry complaining about anything that caught her jaundiced attention.

Jim Steet was buried in the same plot as Lizzie – much against the protests of the Ruanes – but they were quietly told that it had been decided this was the correct thing to do and there was no discussion. Q5 paid the costs from one of their more opaque accounts.

Keane finished reading the file and put it down on the table. He sighed as he went over the events of that night once again.

What a case!

True, Jim Steet had found who killed Lizzie, but it had not done him any good. And the report just underlined that fact.

Keane walked over to the window and looked out, reflecting on the events of those intense hours.

In the garden below, the lawn was white, the trees white, the flowerbeds white. The summer colours hidden and washed out by the sweeping snows that had covered all of the northern heights of London in the past days.

And he turned away from the window, and went to his desk. He picked up his pipe, already filled and ready.

And when he lit it, the smoke curled up like a signal that marked the end of a very closed affair in the street with its envy-filled inhabitants and their bitter lives.

AN EPILOGUE

Much later, a man stood by the grave of Lizzie Ruane. Or Lizzie Steet if you wanted to be more accurate. He had grey, sparse hair and was slightly stooped. And his skin was the unhealthy pallor of someone who had spent a long time indoors, never seeing the sun.

Which was true, because Tristan Thorpe had spent years in prison for two murders. Or, to be legally correct, one murder and one manslaughter.

He stood for a long time by her grave. In his hands was a bunch of bright summer flowers. He put them on the granite surface, his hands trembling a little as they often did nowadays.

After a while he looked up, past the cemetery boundary, across the London skyline to the low hills in the far distance. In between his viewpoint and the horizon, what the Sunday newspaper called 'all human life' was spread out in front of him.

Now it was all over. Truly the end of the affair. Perhaps that Inspector had been right ... what was his name? Oh, yes, Inspector Keane.

Yes, he had been right – Tristan had been too close to it. Always too close to Lizzie in his dreams - but too far away in reality - a dangerous combination.

He preferred to think that she had been a victim of the envy of most of those in the street – that was surely one thing they all had in common - that and their ability to hate.

He thought back to the beginning of it all and remembered a girl in the playground when he was young. A girl who, even in those days, looked destined to break hearts.

He thought of her more than ever now that he was alone.

He remembered a slight fair-haired girl holding his hand in the playground, sharing her lunchtime sandwich with him.

Then the same girl standing shyly across the hall from Jim Steet and him as they stood as near as they dared to the girls at the school dance.

She stood with her friends equally uncertain, looking like an American prom queen. Although in those far off days, they only had a vague idea what a prom queen was, let alone what one looked like.

And, later still, seeing her going out with Jim while he could only watch and envy the casual ease with which Jim treated Lizzie.

And he saw her that night they … well, he did not dare reminisce about it, even in his own mind.

Finally, that day when he went to say goodbye to her and they shared a farewell toast to friendship … then she smiled and closed her eyes and gently leaned forward, silent and quite dead.

He had left her like that – he did not want to touch her. It was the Ruanes who arranged her on the settee and left the note from Jim.

He had not wanted to frame Jim. But once the wheels of the law had been set in motion, and Jim was accused and found guilty … well he was guilty in one sense, and it was only fair that Jim should have had to die for stealing Lizzie from him. Yes, only fair.

Had Jim stayed in prison, he would not have died that night at his attempt at a re-trial. But he'd re-opened wounds that had barely healed and come back to the house, peeling back the layers of envy, of hate, of jealousy.

Because of that, Tristan had no choice but to exact the proper penalty from him.

He turned at last from the grave and walked slowly, carefully, down the gravel path that led to the cemetery entrance.

But in his mind's eye he did not see the path. Instead, he saw – or thought he saw – the figure of Lizzie, thin and almost invisible, as she had appeared in the newspaper pictures.

The newspapers that also mentioned her modelling those famous hands for fashion magazines and detergent advertisements.

And in the bitter end, just her face in the pulp paper coverage of the murder trial. Blurred. Indistinct. Dead.

Yet somewhere behind all that, the same little girl he had once known.

And as he reached the busy road outside the cemetery gates, he saw the rush hour cars driving - a solid stream - on their way home to their houses and their wives - no doubt girls they had known when young, had romanced, and then married.

Something Tristan could only envy.

And the car windscreen wipers weren't moving, yet it seemed to be raining. At least, his vision seemed to be blurred and his eyes were damp.

He set off across the busy road without seeing very well, without looking, without caring very much anymore.